Eye
Candy

Eye Candy

R. L. Stine

BALLANTINE BOOKS • NEW YORK

This is a work of fiction. Names, characters, places, and incidents are the products of the author's imagination or are used fictitiously. Any resemblance to actual events, locales, or persons, living or dead, is entirely coincidental.

A Ballantine Book
Published by The Random House Publishing Group

Copyright © 2004 by R. L. Stine

All rights reserved under International and Pan-American Copyright Conventions. Published in the United States by Ballantine Books, an imprint of The Random House Publishing Group, a division of Random House, Inc., New York, and simultaneously in Canada by Random House of Canada Limited, Toronto.

Ballantine and colophon are registered trademarks of Random House, Inc.

www.ballantinebooks.com

ISBN 978-0-345-46693-8

Manufactured in the United States of America

First Edition: October 2004

OPM 9 8

To Jane, my own eye candy

PART ONE

1

I don't like the way you're looking at me," she said.

I lowered my cup of coffee. I kept my eyes on her. "Like how?"

"Like *that*. Sort of . . . intense."

I smiled. "I'm an intense sort of guy, Alesha."

She spun her cup between her hands, returning my stare. "What do you do, anyway?"

"This and that. Actually, I'm a Web site developer. You know. The tech side."

No point in telling her the truth at this point.

She had coffeecake crumbs on her bottom lip. I wanted to lick them off. She had a nice, full mouth. I liked her eyes, too. Gray-green with yellow flecks, like sunshine.

She licked her lips clean. "Did you work on the dating Web site? You know. The one where we met?"

I shook my head. "Not that one. But I worked on some others. Consulting, mostly."

Consulting sounds like hot shit.

I could see her thinking, "He must be pretty successful." She narrowed her eyes, trying to decide how much I make.

She had a pretty face, with those great eyes and that pouty, full mouth. I'd seen her as soon as I walked into Starbucks, and I'd hoped she was Alesha.

Please—not the one with the ring in her nose, I'd thought. I can't stand that. It makes my whole face hurt to think about it. And when I talk to someone with a pierced tongue, it takes all my willpower not to heave my lunch.

When Alesha turned out to be the pretty one, I almost cheered. I've done a lot of these Internet dating hook-ups, and so far I've been pretty lucky. No Kennel Club members, if you know what I mean.

"What are you thinking about?" Alesha's voice broke into my thoughts.

I pushed my finger through a tiny puddle of water on the table. "How about some dinner?"

She tilted her head, as if she had to consider it. "Well . . . okay. Great."

It was only supposed to be a coffee date. You know, a meet-and-greet kinda thing. But I could tell she was into me. And I just kept staring at those dark red lips. I pictured them doing all kinds of things to me.

A squirrely-looking guy with long strands of greasy, brown hair leaned over the table next to us, banging away on a laptop. Was that supposed to be impressive or something? Why couldn't he do it at home? He's wireless . . . and he's clueless, I thought, as Alesha and I squeezed past him.

We stepped out onto Broadway. I let her go first so I could check out her ass. Not bad. She was wearing those low-riding black pants—not too tight but tight enough.

The wind gusted, blowing her chestnut hair back. It was cold for May, no real sign of spring except for the cherry and apple trees in Riverside Park going all pink and white. It had rained earlier, and the sidewalk was still puddled and shiny.

She struggled to pull her hair into place. "Where do you want to go to eat?"

"We're almost to Eighty-eighth Street. Let's try to get into Aix," I said.

She frowned. "It's always so crowded."

"It's early. Maybe we'll get lucky." I flashed her my best smile. "I'm a lucky kinda guy."

She smiled back with that lovely mouth. Another strong gust flapped my raincoat and blew back the canvas bag she was carrying. She pulled it close to her, and that's when I first noticed her hands, and I felt a little sick inside.

Hands like a truck driver.

I took her to dinner anyway, but now I was a little off my game. I kept glancing at her hands, and I knew the current was going against me.

We sat at a red banquette near the back. She kept her hands below the table, and I made it through dinner. Actually, it was pleasant. I tried hard to revive.

She ordered a glass of some blush wine, and I asked for a Ketel One on the rocks. I could see her expression change when I ordered it. *Maxim* had it on their ten-most-impress-others list, and I trust them.

The restaurant filled up quickly. It's hard to find good gourmet food on the West Side of New York, so this place caught on fast. I bring women here a lot, and they always like it.

The middle-aged couple in the next banquette were arguing loudly over whether to get their dog clipped. The old guy was so heated about not trimming the dog, I thought he might stroke out or something.

"So I'm a nurse," Alesha said, after the food arrived—lamb chops for me, soft-shelled crabs for her. A little early in the season for soft-shelled crabs, if you ask me. "I'm at Roosevelt. You know. Here on the West Side."

"Yeah, I know," I said, salting my chops. "From your profile online. You wrote that you're a nurse. Does that mean you can get all the drugs you want?"

She laughed. She thought I was joking.

I hated her laugh. It was Mom's laugh exactly.

Uh-oh. Mom's laugh and those Hulk Hogan hands. I knew where this evening was heading.

She kept putting her big hand on top of mine, squeezing my skin, smiling at me with those beautiful lips, giving me the look. You know. The look that says, "We're going to end up in my apartment."

Which we did.

It was only a couple of blocks away on Ninetieth and Amsterdam. A pretty big place, airy, with high ceilings, but shabby. The furniture must have come off the street, and nothing interesting hung on the faded walls, just a framed museum print, some Van Gogh thing I've seen a million times.

"How old are you anyway?" Alesha asked, narrowing those eyes at me.

"Twenty-five." This time I told the truth.

"An older man," she whispered. "I'm twenty-three." And then she started kissing me, kissing my face, her lips warm and kinda spongey. Kissing me and making these soft, moaning sounds, biting my ear and holding me, those big mitts against my back.

She pulled me into her bedroom. We sat at the foot of her bed. A blue-and-white quilt in a Quaker design spread out on the bed. A tiny TV almost lost in the piles of clutter on her dresser.

She's so hot. Kissing me and whispering my name.

I could overlook the laugh. But the hands just made me sick.

"Yes, yes," I whispered. "Alesha . . . yes . . ."

I wrapped my hands around her throat. Gently at first, and then I began to squeeze.

I brought my thumbs up and pressed them hard into her larynx. It took her so long to realize what was happening, and then it was too late.

I pressed my thumbs in hard and tightened my hands.

She had no air. Her eyes bulged wide and gazed up at me, as if she was asking me a question. But she had no air. And she couldn't struggle for long. My hands are so strong, and the thumbs do the damage very quickly.

She went limp and stopped breathing.

She was dead but I kept squeezing . . . squeezing. My

hands hurt but I kept squeezing. Because I wanted her eyes to pop out. Just like in the cartoons. I love cartoons. I think they're so funny. If I had a little brother, I'd sit and watch cartoons with him, and we'd both laugh till we peed.

But Mom only had me.

I squeezed till I couldn't squeeze anymore, but the eyes didn't pop. I knew Alesha would disappoint me. What a shame.

I let go and her body collapsed onto the quilt. I struggled to catch my breath. My heart was pounding in my chest. I hadn't been to the gym for a few days. Guess I should go more often.

After a minute or so, I began to feel normal. I hoisted myself off the edge of the bed, clenched and unclenched my hands, trying to work the pain out. Then I stepped into the small, windowless kitchen, no bigger than a closet.

She didn't have much of a knife collection. But I found a serrated bread knife I figured would do the job. Rubbing the blade gently against my thumb, I returned to the bedroom, steamy now. I hadn't noticed the ugly flowered wallpaper.

I held the knife in my right hand and grabbed one of her hands in my left. The hand was limp, the arm heavy. I struggled to get a good grip. Then I began sawing off her fingers, one by one.

I finished the right hand, then went to work on the left. She didn't bleed very much, I guess because she was dead. The fingers felt like asparagus. Real easy to cut.

I realized I had a big smile on my face, so wide my cheeks hurt. Now you have nice small hands, I thought.

But what to do with the fingers?

I counted them—eight fingers. I didn't want the thumbs.

I couldn't decide where to put them, so I jammed them into my raincoat pocket. I left a note, explaining why she had to die. I didn't mention her laugh, just the big hands.

Then I hurried out of the building, a light rain starting to fall, the wind still gusting. I made my way home to my apartment and sat down at the computer without even taking off my raincoat.

Back to the personals site where I found Alesha. After all, there are plenty more women looking for a good time. . . .

2

Is this going to be the most boring date I've ever been on?

Would a cold sore be more fun?

Brain liposuction?

I had a lot of time to think about these questions as I struggled to stay awake. I must have fidgeted a lot because at the intermission Jack said, "Lindy, do you want to leave the theater?"

And of course I wasn't brave enough to say what I really want to do is set my hair on fire and run up the aisle singing "I Enjoy Being a Girl" just to get over my boredom.

So, I said, "No, I'm enjoying it. It's really . . . interesting." I covered my yawn. I don't think he saw it. "Great idea for a musical," I added.

O, America! It was sort of the U.S. Constitution set to music.

"How did you ever get such good seats?" I asked. The theater was half empty. I was trying to be a good sport here. I really was.

"I got 'em for free," Jack said. "At my dad's company where I work. We do marketing for the production company."

After that, I didn't know what to say. So I pretended to read my program. I don't think anyone has ever read a playbill so thoroughly. I could even tell you which Italian restaurant Bernadette Peters recommends.

"I'm working on a really nifty marketing project," Jack said, when I raised my head from the program for air. "I'll tell you all about it at dinner."

Oh, right. Dinner.

Why did I pick this guy? I should have guessed he might be a tad boring from his name. I mean, Jack Smith?

When he picked me up at my apartment lobby, I made a joke. I asked, "What's your *real* name?"

He narrowed his eyes at me. I could see he was surprised by the question, as if no one had ever asked that before.

"That *is* my name, Lindy. Well, actually, I'm Jack Smith the Third, but I don't use that."

Three Jack Smiths in his family?

"What's your middle name?"

"I don't have one."

Figures.

I guess I picked him because he had a nice smile in his photo. Jack isn't a bad-looking guy, actually. He has crinkly blue eyes (I'm a sucker for eyes that crinkle up at the sides), short, brown hair spiked up a bit just in front, and that winning, reassuring smile. Plus he turned out to be almost as tall as I am.

I'm five-eleven, so believe me, size matters. I just feel so awkward when I can reach down and pat my date on the head.

Well, I made it through the second act of *O, America!*, hoping I didn't snore too loudly. When it ended, Jack jumped to his feet, applauding wildly, shaking his head in awe. . . . I guess. Everyone else stood up to put their jackets on and leave. The reaction wasn't terribly enthusiastic, but Jack didn't seem to notice.

We stepped out into a chilly night. The wind blew pages of a newspaper down the sidewalk. I was wearing a red linen vest jacket, open over a sleeveless white T-shirt, and matching red linen pants, and I wished I'd picked out something warmer.

We were halfway through May and, so far, the city hadn't any spring at all. Depressing weather, especially when you don't have a guy you really care about to snuggle up to.

I took Jack's arm, mainly for warmth. He led me past a group of people, middle-aged and older, huddled at the stage door. The door swung open, and a shaggy-looking bear of a man in a gray sweatshirt and black overalls stepped out. Was he Ben Franklin or Cotton Mather? I didn't recognize him. But the small crowd of fans cheered and surged forward to greet him.

"I love New York!" I gushed.

"It's too crowded," was Jack's reply.

Leaning into the wind, we walked up Eighth Avenue,

past small groups of people, all desperately trying to wave down taxis.

"Where are we going for dinner?" I asked.

"My dad's company does some work for this great Italian place on Forty-sixth. I think you'll like it."

Another freebie.

I'm not exactly the Material Girl. But you'd think Jack might have spent at least a dollar or two on our first date.

But hey, the restaurant turned out to be the very one that Bernadette Peters recommended!

Momma Mangia's was long and narrow, the red walls covered with framed paintings of Italian villages. Two rows of tables, each with a red-and-white checkered tablecloth, stretched to the back wall. At a front table, people were toasting one another loudly, clinking glasses and laughing uproariously.

The hostess had trouble finding Jack's reservation. Finally, she led us to a table next to the kitchen door. Two men stopped talking to their wives and watched me as I lowered myself into my seat.

I'm used to it. When you're tall and blond, you notice men watching you. You can feel their eyes on you without even looking. I guess I'm lucky. I mean, would I like it better if they didn't look? I doubt it.

As soon as we sat down, a white-aproned waiter leaned over the table and, in a very heavy Italian accent, asked if we'd like a drink. A totally phony accent. He had to be an out-of-work actor. I ordered a glass of red wine, to warm up, and Jack ordered a Diet Coke.

Jack clasped his hands on the tabletop and leaned closer. He grinned at me. "That play got me all psyched. I mean, I'm not the most patriotic guy. But those songs . . . they really made me feel something."

Was he for real?

"Tell me about your exciting project," I said. Clever change of subject?

He unclasped his hands, then clasped them again. He had very smooth, large hands, I noticed. Very well-groomed. "It's the biggest assignment I've had since I joined Dad's firm."

"How old are you anyway, Jack?" I interrupted.

"I'll be twenty-six in July."

"So I'm out with an older man. That could be danger-ous," I teased, squeezing his hand.

He didn't pick up on it at all. "Why? How old are you, Lindy?"

"Twenty-three."

And going on 110 tonight!

He nodded. "My sister is twenty-three."

So what?

"It's for Cat Chow," he said.

I had lost the thread for a moment. "What is?"

"My marketing project."

My hair fell over my face. I swept it back with a shake of my head. I glanced to the next table and saw the two men still staring at me. They looked away when I stared back.

"It's the biggest Cat Chow promotion we've ever done, see. And Dad tossed it in my lap."

I pictured Dad tossing a cat into his lap. My face started to itch. I'm allergic to cats.

"And here's my great idea," Jack said, his eyes going bright, his whole face suddenly alive. "I thought of it while I was watching cartoons. You know. Sylvester the Cat and his little cat son."

"You watch cartoons, Jack?"

He nodded excitedly. Eager to tell me his big Cat Chow idea. "I call it The Whisker Walk."

He raised two fingers on each hand to the sides of his face, like little cat whiskers, and he began moving the "whiskers" up and down in a little dance while he meowed a little song.

That's when I faded out. Or rather, that's when Jack faded out.

I didn't hear another word he said. I just kept picturing him meowing and doing his little Whisker Walk with his fingers. Would I ever be able to forget it? Where is a rewind button when you need it?

O, America! O, America! I had no idea the play would be the best part of the evening.

How did I get into this? Why am I going out with guys I meet on the Internet? After all, Jack isn't the first. Last week was Brad. And next week will be Colin. And here's what I *don't* know as I sit here pretending to listen to Jack . . . here's a little detail I haven't learned yet . . .

One of the three guys is a murderer. One of them plans to murder *me*.

I'll find this out really soon. And then, here's the punch line: The only way I'll stay alive is to keep going out with all three of them.

A nightmare? Yes, and it's only beginning. How did I get myself into this mess? I'll tell you. I guess it started the night Ben was killed.

3

When Tommy Foster called to tell me Ben was killed in a car chase, shot like in the movies, his squad car spinning into a wall, I didn't react at all. I held the phone to my ear, pressed it there with all my might, listening for more. Listening for something real.

Things like that only happen to other people, right?

Ben had this car-chase PlayStation game. He was so into it, playing it endlessly, almost as if his life depended on it. I'm not looking for irony or anything. It's just when Lieutenant Foster, Ben's partner, called with the news—long pauses between each word, his voice trembling, a sob escaping his throat—the first thing I thought about was that game.

The game was real. But Ben dead? That *couldn't* be real.

Ben and I were a golden couple. It may sound immodest, but I'm being honest. People gasped when Ben and I walked into a room. He was tall and blond like me, and had a rolling walk and a trim, athletic body, and those blue eyes that reflected the sunlight.

Golden.

We had nearly a year. I met him at my gym, and we started goofing on each other and kidding around. One day we had a treadmill race, an intense competition until my heart pounded and my legs ached, and finally, we both collapsed into each other's arms, laughing and sweating on each other, gasping for breath.

We stayed in each other's arms from then on.

You could have cast us in a movie. A love story. I was the savvy New Yorker, spent my whole life in middle-class luxury in Manhattan, even college at NYU. He was a New Jersey guy, from a big Italian family, a family of cops for generations.

But don't get me wrong. There weren't any clichés here. He was shrewd and funny, taught courses at John Jay, liked movies and plays, even the opera when we could scrounge up two tickets.

No matter how long the line, dance club bouncers always held the rope aside when Ben and I appeared. Because we were golden.

When Ben died, the light in my life went out. I lived in blues and grays, the colors of that dark video game where the cars squealed after each other, crashed and disintegrated.

And now, nearly a year later, spring approaching, another lonely summer staring me in the face—another summer with the girls—and I was pacing back and forth in front of my roommates in the narrow living-room of our apartment.

Ann-Marie sat cross-legged on the carpet, punching

in numbers on her new cell phone. She'd left the old one on the subway, and now it was like she had to start her life all over again.

Luisa sprawled on the brown leather couch, balancing a Diet Coke on her stomach, reading a James Patterson paperback. Ann-Marie and I call Luisa Goth Girl. Not because of her personality (which is a little dark, actually), but because of her raven black hair, straight and thick, almost like a helmet framing her slender, pale face.

"I haven't had a decent date in a year."

The words tumbled from my mouth in a harsh voice I didn't recognize. I had my arms tightly crossed in front of me. I plopped down in the big La-Z-Boy to keep from pacing.

Ann-Marie clicked her phone shut and looked up at me. Luisa kept reading. She raised a finger. "Let me just finish this page."

"Finish the whole book," I snapped. "I'm just babbling."

"Go ahead and babble," Ann-Marie said. "We like it when Miss Universe is a little stressed."

I glared at Ann-Marie. "Don't call me that. That's my whole problem, don't you see? Guys think I'm . . ."

"Too beautiful?" Luisa helped out from the couch.

"I didn't say that. It's just that I've been told I . . . *intimidate* guys. So they don't ask me out."

Ann-Marie laughed. "What a terrible problem, Lindy. Too gorgeous. That one goes right up there with world hunger."

Luisa and I laughed. Ann-Marie always knew how to put things in perspective.

Ann-Marie has short, wavy auburn hair, which I keep urging her to lighten, at least with a few streaks. She has beautiful, olive-colored eyes, but her face is very round and her front teeth poke out a bit, giving her a kind of chipmunky look.

And though I hate to say it, she could probably lose a few pounds. She's a fanatic about the gym, but I think the problem is all the big Italian dinners she's been cooking for her new boyfriend, Lou D'Amici.

Luisa closed her book and turned to me. "Can't you meet any guys at your office?"

"Are you kidding?" I cried. "I work in children's publishing. There *are* no guys in children's publishing!"

I thought about my office, all women except for Saralynn's assistant, Brill, who is gay.

Luisa casually ran a hand through her dark bangs. "Lindy, you could hang out at any bar. Slap on a short skirt and a tube top, show off your legs and let your tits hang out, and you'll meet a dozen guys a night."

I sighed. "No offense, but I don't want to meet guys in bars."

She sneered at me. "Snob."

Luisa waitresses at The Spring Street Bar in SoHo, and she's always bringing guys home after work. I see them creeping out of her room in the morning, smiles on their faces.

"I'm not a snob," I said. "I don't want to meet guys who like me for my body. Guys looking for another dumb blonde. You know I'm right, Luisa. I want someone I can talk to."

"Well, why don't you do what I did?" Ann-Marie asked, repeatedly flipping her cell phone open and shut.

I frowned at her. "Write a personals ad?"

She grinned. "Worked for me."

"She's right. Lou is a great guy," Luisa said, opening her book again. "You should do it, Lindy. Meet-Market.com."

"Yeah, I got so many replies," Ann-Marie said, climbing to her feet. "You remember. We picked Lou out because he crossed his eyes in his photo. We figured he had to have a sense of humor."

"Or else he was cross-eyed," I said.

"He's funny," Luisa said. "He always cracks me up."

"He's sweet, too," Ann-Marie said, her cheeks turning pink. "Did you see those earrings he bought me? He said they were undiamonds for my unbirthday."

"I think they were real zircons," I joked.

Ann-Marie didn't laugh. She doesn't like jokes about Lou. Maybe I'm a little jealous of her. She's so crazy about him.

"Anyone want an apple or something?" Ann-Marie disappeared into the kitchen.

"I couldn't write an ad about myself," I said. "It would be too embarrassing. What would I say? 'I like long walks in the moonlight on winding country roads? I want someone who's honest and sincere and likes me just for me?' Puke."

Ann-Marie returned carrying a slice of cheesecake

on a plate. "Left over from dinner with Lou last night," she explained, swallowing a mouthful.

"Ann-Marie will write the ad for you," Luisa said. "She's batting a thousand."

"Yeah, sure. No problem," Ann-Marie said. "I'll write the ad. I know just what to say."

The next day, she showed me the ad she had placed on the Web site, and I was horrified.

4

Eye Candy?" I screamed. "Ann-Marie—how could you call me *Eye Candy?"*

I blinked at the laptop screen, hoping the ad would magically change. But there I still was, smiling out at myself above the boldfaced headline: EYE CANDY.

Ann-Marie sat in the desk chair, eyes on the laptop. I stood behind her. I wrapped my hands around her neck and pretended to strangle her. "Aaaaagh! How could you do this to me?"

"Give me a break, Lindy." She pried my hands from her neck. "Everyone puts in a funny name to describe themselves."

"But *Eye Candy?"*

"Take a breath, okay. Let's face it, you're beautiful, right? You're drop-dead gorgeous, no kidding. It's a perfect name for you."

"But . . . yuck. It sounds like bragging. Who's going to want to go out with a girl who calls herself Eye Candy?"

Ann-Marie shrugged. "You'll see . . ."

Lou appeared in the doorway. He lumbered into the bedroom, followed by Luisa.

Lou is very tall. He ducks his head under every doorway. He's big, too, not fat, just what they call big-boned, I guess. He wears size 13 shoes. He can't enter a room quietly. The floorboards creak under him. Sometimes when he gives Ann-Marie a big hug, I expect to hear her ribs crack.

"Hey, what's up?" He leaned down and kissed Ann-Marie on the cheek.

"We have a little problem," I said. "Check this out." I pointed to the laptop.

Lou bumped Ann-Marie off the chair and sat down. He leaned toward the screen, his thick, black eyebrows moving up and down as he read my ad.

I stepped up beside him. "It's terrible, right?"

He turned and slid his arm around my waist. "*I'd* go out with you!"

Ann-Marie let out a growl and gave Lou a hard shove. "You creep!" She balled up her hands and began punching him.

He laughed and ducked behind his hands to block her punches. "Give me a break, Annie! She asked for an opinion!"

Ann-Marie shoved him again.

"Eye Candy, huh?" Lou said, turning back to the screen. "Whose idea was that?"

"It wasn't mine!" I said.

"Mine," Ann-Marie said. "And I think it's perfect for Lindy."

"And look what else she wrote," I said, as Lou scrolled down the screen. "She wrote that I'm a publishing executive. What a total lie!"

"Of course you're a publishing executive," Ann-Marie insisted.

"I'm an editorial assistant," I said. "Why did you have to exaggerate?"

Ann-Marie crossed her arms in front of her. "Everyone exaggerates a little."

"You didn't exaggerate about the eye candy part," Lou chimed in, grinning. He ducked as Ann-Marie began to punch him again.

"You really like getting beat up, don't you, Lou?" Luisa said.

He grabbed Ann-Marie's hands to stop her attack. "I'm into all kinds of kinky things," he said. "You'd be surprised."

I suddenly had a picture in my mind—Lou in handcuffs, chained to the bed, Ann-Marie straddling him, raining little punches down on him.

Whoa.

"Are you sure this is safe?" Luisa asked, gazing down at my photo on the screen. "I mean, putting yourself out on the Internet like that. Aren't there a lot of creeps out there?"

Lou laughed. "You mean me?"

Luisa's dark eyes flashed. "No, even worse than you."

Ann-Marie frowned. "Lindy's a big girl. She'll know if a guy is okay or not."

5

I don't read the fucking *New York Times*. Too many words, and it doesn't fit on my breakfast table. People make fun of the *Post* because it's a tabloid, but it tells me everything I need to know. I sip my coffee and flip through it every morning before work, with *NY1 News* on the TV in the background. You know. "Weather on the Ones." You can't beat it.

It was a rainy morning, the third straight. My apartment windows were all spattered and streaked, and I was staring out at the soupy gray. Kinda depressing when you're waiting for spring to start.

I was thinking about work and how I'd rather go back to bed and maybe watch one of my new porno DVDs. Then I nearly dropped my fucking coffee cup when I caught the headline on the top of page four.

WEST-SIDE WOMAN STRANGLED IN HER APT.

Tell me about it. My hands were still sore from squeezing so hard.

I pictured her eyes going big when she realized what was happening. And again I heard the startled gasp she made when my thumbs began to press on her voice box. Her head went back. And the hoarse, gurgling sounds she made at the end were pretty gross.

I set down my cup and pulled the newspaper to my face with both hands and read the article slowly and carefully. What was her name again? Alesha Morgan? I'd nearly forgotten. And yeah, yeah. I remembered she'd said she was a nurse.

I should have asked her more questions, gotten to know her a little better.

I read the article twice from beginning to end. I mean, it's exciting being in the newspaper. It didn't mention anything about her missing fingers.

What kind of reporting is that?

How could the guy not notice her fingers were missing?

Maybe it's some kind of police trick. I've read about how they hold certain details back. Some kind of trap for suspects.

Well, I had the fingers right on the breakfast table beside the paper. I picked them up and squeezed them in my hand. They'd turned brown and gotten kinda hard and brittle. Like dried out pea pods. I slapped them against the tabletop, pounding out a rhythm. They made a nice sound.

I used to be a drummer. We had a jazz band in college. Big band stuff, very retro, and I had a nice, light touch on the snare. I liked playing brushes, not pounding the sticks. After all, I'm an easygoing kinda guy.

I put four fingers in one hand and four fingers in the

other, and I began drumming the table. I guess I had a lot of pent-up energy. It's kind of exciting being in the paper. *Ba beba bebaba bada bada bam bam*.

When the phone rang, I tossed the fingers into the air and shouted, *"Olé."*

"Oh, hi, Mom. How's it going? Yeah. I'm just on my way out the door."

She calls any hour of the day or night. She thinks I have no life. She means well, but she still thinks she has to take care of me. She didn't take care of me much when I was a kid, so I guess she's trying to make up for things.

"You tried me last night? When did you call, Ma?"

Around nine.

"I had a date. I was out with a very beautiful, young woman. A nurse. Yeah. You shouldn't try me at night, Ma. I go out almost every night of the week."

Am I overdoing it? Wearing myself out?

"What can I do, Ma? The women don't leave me alone. Hey, don't worry about me. I'm enjoying life, you know. You're only old once, right? Isn't that what you always said? So I might as well have a good time before I get old and decrepit like you. Ha ha. Only joking. I know, I know. You're forty-nine and you don't have a wrinkle. Yeah, you told me that a few times."

What else is new?

"Well, I'm thinking of getting a tattoo. A big blue-and-red-winged demon on my chest. Ha ha. No. Only kidding, Ma. Just wanted to hear you scream."

Work?

"Work is great. I'm making enough money to keep up my glam lifestyle. No, seriously. People are starting to take notice. Listen, I'll tell you something great. There was a story about me in the paper this morning. No. Really. In the *New York Post*. A really nice piece. Maybe I'll send it to you."

A few more blah-blah-blahs, and I said goodbye to her and clicked off the phone. I stuck my fingers in my ears for some silence. She has a shrill, scratchy voice. It always takes me a few minutes to get it out of my head.

After a moment or so, I stood up and crossed to the front window. It was a short walk. My condo isn't very big. I'm kinda cramped. But at least the place is easy to take care of.

I squinted through the spattered window. The rain had stopped. The clouds were lifting. Things were looking up.

I'll go back online tonight, I told myself. Something to look forward to all day. Yes, I'll go back to that personals site tonight, maybe find a hot new girlfriend.

6

Check out this guy," Ann-Marie said, poking her finger at the laptop screen. "Oh, wow. A snake tattoo on his cheek. This guy's your type, Lindy."

"Look at his eyes," Luisa leaned over me, one hand on my shoulder, the other hand holding a can of Budweiser. "He is totally trashed. I'll bet he hasn't been sober since junior high school."

Ann-Marie grinned. "I dare you to go out with him, Lindy. How about it?"

"No way." I scrolled down to the next one.

A few days after the Eye Candy ad went online, I had dozens of answers. Now I sat in front of the laptop, my roommates huddled around me, reading the replies, the three of us hooting with laughter, sometimes shaking our heads in disbelief.

I scrolled past a boy who looked about fourteen but claimed to be twenty-five and bragged that he drove a red Hummer.

Luisa sipped her beer. "Maybe he has a red Hummer tricycle." She and Ann-Marie burst out laughing.

"You two are enjoying this too much," I grumbled. "You think it's some kind of game. But it's my *life*!"

"We're only trying to help you," Ann-Marie insisted. "Whoa. Stop. You're going too fast. Look at this one."

"Celebrity I Most Look Like: 'Tobey Maguire.' "

Luisa leaned closer to the screen. "Ohmigod. Poor guy. He *does* look like Tobey Maguire. Hey, what if it *is* Tobey Maguire and he replied to your ad and said the celeb he resembles most is Tobey Maguire. Wouldn't that be pitiful?"

I laughed. "Lu, we know you're from another planet, but you should try to hide it sometimes."

She pressed the cold beer can against the back of my neck, and I let out a squeal.

Ann-Marie was gazing at "Tobey." "Here's your chance to go out with a movie star—or a movie star lookalike," Ann-Marie said.

"Pass," I said. "Too short. I'd have to lift him over big puddles."

Ann-Marie put on her serious face. "Okay, okay. We're looking for tall here. Stop. Check out this guy."

R U HOT ENUF?

"And look. He has it right on his T-shirt." I jabbed my finger at the screen. "R U HOT ENUF?"

"Bet he had that done special for him at the mall," Luisa said. "I like the spiked-up hair. Where's his skateboard?"

"And read this," Ann-Marie added. *"Reason to Get to Know Me: '9 inches.' "*

"Too subtle," I said.

I scrolled down to what had to be the most pitiful one of all. I let out a moan. "I don't believe this."

BIG FAT LOSER.

I stared at his photo. Well, at least he was honest.

And underneath the photo, he had written: *"Won't you help me find my good qualities?"*

"It makes you want to cry," I said. "The guy's looking for a sympathy date."

Luisa snickered. "A mercy killing would be better."

The next one was a possible.

"Jack Smith?" Ann-Marie narrowed her eyes at the screen. "That can't be his real name, can it?"

"It might be," I said, scanning his reply. Very normal and sincere. He didn't seem crazy.

I sighed. Ben suddenly flashed into my mind. Like he was watching me. And how did I feel? Embarrassed. Looking for guys on the Internet while he . . .

Ben was gone, except for those moments when I saw him smiling at me from somewhere. Here's a secret: I kept the car-chase video game. I have it in my underwear drawer. Part of him is still with me, or something like that. I know it's stupid.

Luisa drained the beer can and crushed it in her hand. "What if your name was Jack Smith, and your whole life no one believed you?"

"And what if you looked like Tobey Maguire?" Ann-Marie added. "And had nine inches and drove it around in a red Hummer? Then you'd be totally cool, right?"

I sighed. "You two aren't helping me at all." I nodded to the screen. "This guy is a possible maybe."

Luisa made a face. "He's so straight. Like he works in the towel department at Bed, Bath & Beyond."

Luisa is a strange girl, but I mean that in a good way. I'll never forget how we met. Someone at her office gave Ann-Marie tickets to a blues concert at the Beacon Theatre on Broadway. We weren't really into blues, but we had nothing better to do, so we went.

The show started about an hour late, and Luisa was sitting next to me and we started talking. She was really funny and seemed nice, and was really into blues music, which she talked about with amazing enthusiasm.

Ann-Marie and I were looking for a third roommate. We already had an ad in the *Village Voice* and on *Craig's List*. We had this big apartment at Seventy-ninth and Amsterdam, and our other roommate went home to Ohio, so we desperately needed a third person to help pay the rent, or we'd be hitting the streets.

Luisa had a sublet in the Village that was almost up. So, it seemed karma was on our side. She's been with us for nearly a year. But we don't see her that much since she works such long hours at the bar.

"You're really going to email Jack Smith?" Ann-Marie asked.

I nodded. "Yeah. I think so. Check him out. There's something nice about his eyes."

And that's how I ended up at *O, America!* as Jack's freebie date, watching him do the Whisker Dance and thinking about *101 Ways to Kill a Cat,* a book my older brother thought was hilarious.

Besides Jack, I found two other guys to reply to.

Colin O'Connor was really good-looking, with wavy dark hair, a great smile, and a dimple under his chin. He wrote that he was a mortgage banker, but *"please don't hold it against me."* He was one of the few guys who'd replied who wasn't wearing a T-shirt in his photo.

I also wrote back to Brad Fisher. He said he had been a journalism major and was working as a reporter for one of the weekly give-away newspapers. His note was really funny. He wrote that he was looking for *"someone who hates long walks in the moonlight, can't dance, has no sense of humor, and doesn't care about the whales."*

Kind of irresistible.

"So it's Jack, Colin, and Brad," I said to my roommates. "I don't have high hopes. But maybe one of them will turn out to be fun."

Luisa snorted. "You're crazy. You picked the three most boring guys."

"Don't listen to her," Ann-Marie said. "You'll find someone terrific, Lin. I know you will." She hugged me from behind.

"Maybe you should go out with all three of them at once," Luisa said. "That might make it more interesting. Or maybe pick five or six of them. Big Fat Loser, too."

"Luisa, please—"

"Yes! This is awesome. You tell them it's a TV show. Like on Fox," Luisa continued. "You chain them all to you, and they follow you everywhere. That way, you really get to know them. And then each week, you have a vote. Everyone votes, and you eliminate the most obnoxious one."

The idea had us all laughing. It was a riot.

But the fun ended quickly.

It ended with one phone call.

7

I went out with Brad Fisher first. He was almost as tall as me, a wiry, thin guy, lots of energy. He had a birdlike look to him, a beaky nose that had been broken a few times in playground fights, he said. He brought it up—I didn't. His round brown eyes were perched very close together, close to his broken nose.

I liked his crooked smile. He talked out of the side of his mouth, like a gangster, and he could dangle a cigarette from his lips and talk at the same time, something I know he learned at the movies.

We got along pretty well, even though we didn't have a chance to talk much. He took me to Blondie's, a loud sports bar on Seventy-ninth Street, just a few doors down from my apartment. We split a huge platter of buffalo wings, very hot and spicy, and he had three beers to my one.

We had to shout to be heard over the crowd and the music, so we mainly smiled across the table at each other and kept wiping the barbecue sauce off our cheeks with our napkins.

Then we jumped in a cab, and Brad took me to Caroline's Comedy Club near Times Square to see Colin Quinn and a bunch of other stand-ups complain about their girlfriends and airline stewardesses and how stupid the mayor was.

Brad had another three beers to my one. And before I knew it, we were back uptown in front of my apartment saying goodnight. And I'd hardly learned a thing about him. His parents were Russian immigrants and he grew up near Coney Island, and his first after-school job had been taking tickets for the Cyclone, the famous roller-coaster there. And . . . what else?

What else about Brad? He was working as a reporter at the *New York Weekly,* a free newspaper filled with local news and politics and grocery store ads. But he said he was just doing that for experience. He knew someone at the *Daily News* who had offered to give him a try-out soon. After working in newspapers for a few years, he planned to move to TV news.

And what else?

I can't think of much else.

It was a chilly, damp evening. Spring just refused to arrive, even though it was May. I climbed out of the cab. Brad followed me out and stood with the cab door open behind him, saying goodnight. A car rolled by, one of those huge Suburban SUV's, blaring rap music loud enough for the whole block to enjoy, and I still couldn't hear what Brad was saying.

And then the SUV moved past. Brad held my hand. "You know, guys stare at you wherever you go," he said. "Do you realize that? I mean, guys really look at you."

I didn't know what to say to that, so I said, "Does that bother you?"

He got this strange smile on his face but didn't say anything. And then he raised both hands and grabbed the back of my head.

He wrapped his hands tightly around my hair, and he pulled my face to his. Not gently, but hard. And he kissed me—a hard, dry kiss, pressing his mouth against mine so tightly I could feel his teeth.

It hurt. And I hated the way he held my head in place, like a wrestling hold. And when he opened his mouth and his tongue started to force my lips open, I jerked back. Grabbed his wrists and pulled his hands off my head.

I stumbled over the curb, gasping for breath, my heart pounding. My lips throbbed. Were they bleeding?

Brad stood with a crooked smile on his face. Almost as if nothing had happened. But he was breathing hard, too.

My whole body tensed. I balled my hands into fists. "Listen, Brad—"

"Sorry," he said. "I . . . slipped."

Slipped?

He reached for my hand, but I pulled it away from him.

"I'm a total klutz," he said, avoiding my eyes. "Sorry."

I stared hard at him. Was he for real?

"You coming, Mister?" the cab driver called.

"Hey, I'll email you," Brad said. He didn't give me a chance to reply. He ducked back into the cab. The door slammed shut, and the cab pulled away.

I stood at the curb, licking my cut lip. It throbbed with pain.

Did he really slip? Was he just nervous?

I hurried into my building. Riding up the elevator, I thought about Brad's laugh. Such a loud, showy, angry laugh.

At Caroline's, Brad had laughed loudest at all the totally sexist jokes. He howled at every joke putting women down. And a guy who told joke after joke about blondes—*What kind of word-processing program can a blonde use? A pencil!* Ha ha ha—that guy made Brad roar.

Did he think I was a dumb blonde, too?

Well . . . I felt all mixed up about Brad. I mean, he was cute, like a big stork with that bird face of his and that crooked smile. And he was almost as tall as me. But what was with that kiss?

Now, here we are, one week later, with Jack Smith. We had to get back to him sometime, didn't we?

He's been doing the Whisker Dance and telling me his ideas on how to market Cat Chow. And I've been thinking about Brad, and Ben, and Luisa, and Ann-Marie, thinking about how I got into this, and trying to listen to Jack. I mean, trying to be nice and concentrate on what he's saying, but, come on, Cat Chow just isn't at the top of my Most Fascinating list.

We get out of the restaurant. I'm gulping like a fish for fresh air. "It's such a nice night," Jack says. "Let's walk back to your apartment."

The play was free, dinner was free—and now he doesn't even want to spring for two bucks for the subway to get me back to Seventy-ninth Street?

"I'm feeling kinda wiped," I tell him. "Maybe I'll just jump in the subway over there." I point to Forty-ninth Street. "Where do you live, anyway?"

"Hoboken. Right over the river." He points west. "My dad lets me use a condo he owns. Rent free, do you believe it? It has the greatest view. I mean, why live in Manhattan when you can see it all from the other side?"

"Sounds great," I say, trying to sound convincing.

"Well, I guess this is it," he says, blue eyes crinkling up. Even the crinkling eyes don't win me over now. "I'm heading downtown. You know. The PATH train."

You mean you don't *walk* back to New Jersey? Wow. Big spender.

"Well . . . goodnight, Jack. Thanks for the play and everything."

He nods. "It was great."

Two taxis squeal to the curb. The drivers, both big, burly men in turbans, jump out and begin screaming at each other. They're both waving their fists in the air, bumping each other with their broad chests, cursing each other, screaming, spitting on the pavement.

"I . . . I'd better go," I say.

Jack nods again. We take a few steps away from the battling drivers. A crowd has quickly gathered on the corner to watch the fight.

Jack has to shout over the screaming voices. "Can I call you?"

Oh God. Did I give him my number? I don't remember giving it to him. How did he get it?

I don't want to encourage him. And I don't want to hurt his feelings. He's not a bad guy, really. Especially if you're into marketing for cats . . .

One driver shoves the other onto his back on a taxi hood. They begin pounding their fists at each other. The driver on his back reaches up and pulls off the other's turban. Grunting, cursing, they begin wrestling frantically for the turban, pulling it apart as they struggle. Finally, one of them heaves it into passing traffic, and a speeding SUV rolls over it.

"Jack, I've really got to go."

"So can I call you?"

"Maybe. Why don't you email me?"

I see the disappointment on his face.

Two very young-looking police officers are jogging across Eighth Avenue, holding up their hands to halt traffic, hurrying to stop the fight.

Jack lowers his face to kiss me. I turn my head so his lips brush my cheek.

Again, I see his disappointed expression.

"Bye," he says. He spins away, glances at the battling drivers, then takes off downtown.

Cross him off the list, I tell myself. Dull, dull, dull. He's history.

But nothing is ever that simple, is it?

8

The apartment was smoky and sweet-smelling. The tangy aroma of pot. Lou and Ann-Marie were in a haze, too. Wrapped up together on the livingroom couch, her skirt high on her thighs, one of her bare legs draped over his. A dim light behind them pierced the fog like a distant lighthouse.

Ann-Marie giggled when she saw me. She had Lou's hand in hers and was holding it between her legs. Her hair was wet and frazzled.

She never used to get stoned before she met Lou. She never used to cook up big pans of lasagna and mountains of spaghetti marinara. She never used to go to metal concerts or Vin Diesel movies, either.

Ann-Marie had changed a lot, all on Lou's account, and I was happy for her, truly pleased to see her so glowing. She had been melancholy and depressed during the two years I roomed with her at NYU. No guys in her life. Unhappy because her older sisters were so good-looking and successful, and her parents treated her like she was some mutt they'd found in the pound.

The October they forgot her birthday, I wanted to drive out to Little Neck and strangle them both. Instead, I spent hours trying to get her to stop crying and tearing at her hair and pounding her forehead against the windowpane.

That was the year Ann-Marie decided she wanted a nose job for her birthday. I couldn't talk her out of it. Her nose is perfectly okay. Luckily, she couldn't afford it, and of course her parents wouldn't spend anything on her.

She was so unhappy with her looks, so unhappy over everything about herself, I sometimes had the feeling she'd like to crawl out of her skin completely, leave it behind the way a snake does.

After college, I didn't want to room with her. I wanted someone more stable, a little more fun, less depressed. I guess that makes me sound selfish. But I'd spent two years with Ann-Marie, and I knew we'd stay friends, so I started to make other plans.

But then she found this huge apartment on West Seventy-ninth Street that was actually affordable, mainly because she found a pretty good job as an assistant at a talent management agency in the Village. When she asked me to room with her, I couldn't say no.

Ann-Marie seemed a lot better these days. Being out of all the competition and pressure at NYU freed her, I think, lightened her up. She spent long hours at her job. She liked it because it was kind of glamorous.

The agency had a bunch of TV and music performers as clients—no huge stars, but a lot of names I recognized. Ann-Marie's job was mainly to act as Mom, to take care of them, to get them hotel rooms and make restaurant reservations for them, to be there for them when any problems came up on the road, to make sure there were food baskets in their rooms when they arrived, and whatever they wanted to drink. Occasionally she'd even buy cocaine for them, but we had to get Ann-Marie pretty wasted before she'd loosen up and talk about that part of the job.

So Ann-Marie was in a much better mood, a lot more steady. And when Luisa moved in, she helped, too, because she was just so off-the-wall and funny. And then someone at Ann-Marie's agency told her about Meet-Market.com, she met Lou, and the old, depressed and self-doubting Ann-Marie seemed to disappear completely.

She really did leave her old skin behind.

I tiptoed into the apartment, almost choking on the sweet-sour air. "Sorry to interrupt."

Ann-Marie giggled again.

Lou had his head back on the couch. He raised it as I approached, squinting into the haze, struggling to focus his eyes. I saw the recognition on his face when he finally remembered who I was.

Whew. How stoned do you have to be to be that stoned? Why didn't they save some of it for tomorrow? But, hey, maybe I was just in a pissy mood because Jack turned out to be such a loser.

I had to pass by the couch to get to my room. The ashtray on the coffee table contained little charred specks, the remains of smoked joints. Several empty beer cans lay on their sides on the carpet beside the couch.

"How was . . . whatsisname? Jack?" Ann-Marie asked in a throaty, hoarse voice. She brought Lou's hand up to her face and stroked her cheek with it.

"You don't want to know," I groaned.

"Tell us," Ann-Marie insisted.

"No. Really. Let's not go there. He was pretty bad. I'll tell you tomorrow."

I started past the couch. Lou was sitting up now, and he was staring at my breasts. Leaning over Ann-Marie to ogle my breasts. Not even trying to be subtle about it.

Ann-Marie giggled and leaned into him. Did she notice? Did she see how he was staring at me?

"Why don't you come sit down with us?" Lou asked, grinning. He patted the cushion beside him.

Ann-Marie giggled again and gave him a playful slap on the cheek. "Bad boy."

"Goodnight," I said, and, tripping over beer cans, I hurried to my room.

I closed the door carefully behind me and stood for a long moment in the darkness, catching my breath.

Ann-Marie had to notice Lou staring at my breasts like that. She had to see the way he looked at me.

Now I heard them moaning together, moaning in pleasure on the other side of the door.

Didn't she care?

9

I don't think about guys all the time. I do have a job, you know, as editorial assistant at FurryBear Press. We do the *FurryBear* picturebooks. You've probably seen them. They're even being developed by PBS as a cartoon series—or rather, there's an option on them.

I don't always work on FurryBear, however. Rita Belson, the other editorial assistant, and I work on other titles—individually, because we never could work together. She's such a bitch. You should have seen the look on Rita's face when Saralynn Palmer, our boss and the co-founder of FurryBear, gave me my own book series to work on. Rita practically had a stroke. After all, she's Saralynn's favorite.

People can get pretty childish working in children's publishing, and I don't mean that in a good way. One day last month I was thinking about my problems with Rita and about how competitive everyone was at Furry-Bear. And I remembered someone once said, "Children's books are a bunny-eat-bunny business."

I think about that on the subway every morning on my way to work.

The picturebook series Saralynn gave me to work on is called *Wings to Imagination*. It's about all the winged creatures in the world, and about how birds fly thousands of miles every year when they migrate, and imagining what it would be like if we could do it, too.

I know, I know. It isn't like great literature—hell, it isn't even *FurryBear*—but it was flattering that Saralynn thinks I'm ready to edit a whole series. Especially since she gave the assignment to me in front of Rita.

So, I had other things to think about this week. Plus, my father had gallbladder surgery, and I spent one afternoon in Beth Israel visiting him and listening to him complain about getting old.

But yes, I did think about guys some of the time. I had dates to reminisce about. With Brad and Jack. And still one date to go—Colin O'Connor. I thought a lot about Colin and hoped he'd turn out to be nice. Or even someone I could be crazy about, the way Ann-Marie is crazy about Lou.

Saturday night, still cold, a half moon low in the purple sky over Central Park, I took a bus across town to Second Avenue.

There are bars up and down Second Avenue, sports bars, singles bars, old-timey bars and pubs, many of them with Irish names. But I knew Ryan's on the corner of Sixty-seventh Street from high school days. My Stuyvesant High friends and I used to meet there because the bartenders had a very lenient attitude about carding. It was basically a yuppie hangout, guys in suits three-deep at the bar after work, later giving way to the Dockers-and-Polo-shirt crowd.

Red bricks in front framed a big picture window filled with blinking red and green neon beer signs. Clusters of people leaned against the building, smoking furtively as if they were criminals, smoking quickly, without any enjoyment, getting it out of the way like a quick pee, so they could go back inside to rejoin their friends.

I was wearing a scoop-necked black top, long-sleeved and sheer, over a short, straight white skirt with a skinny, black belt. At the last moment, I thought maybe I was too dressed up for a bar date. So I took off my heels and slipped into a pair of flat, red sandals. And I pulled my hair back into a simple, schoolgirl ponytail.

I could see guys turn to stare at me as I made my way to the entrance to Ryan's. "Yo, are you looking for *me*?" a beefy guy in a blue and orange Mets hoodie shouted. Some other guys laughed.

I didn't turn around. I pushed open the door and stepped inside. That familiar beery smell. My eyes scanned the long, mahogany bar. A wall of shiny, clean glasses glimmered, suspended upside down over the bar. Two of the bartenders were women, wearing tight black tube tops with RYAN'S in white type across their chests.

A TV above the bar showed a Yankees game with the sound off, but no one seemed to be watching. The mostly well-dressed crowd was talking, tilting glasses to their mouths, laughing, hooking up.

Where was Colin?

I stepped away from the bar, side-stepped an aproned waiter holding a tray of glasses and empty bottles above his head, and peered down the row of dark green booths against the far wall.

Yes. A dark-haired guy in a black Polo shirt sat alone at a booth for two. Unsure, I nodded in his direction. He smiled and raised his beer bottle to me.

Nice smile, I thought, as I eased myself into the seat across from him. "Hi, Colin. Sorry I'm late."

He cupped his ear. "Sorry. That woman has the loudest laugh on earth." He pointed to the booth behind him, to a woman with her back turned, bright orange hair cascading down her shoulders.

"I just said 'hi,' " I shouted, leaning across the table.

The woman tossed back her head and laughed again.

He raised his bottle, a Corona with a lime. "Buy you a drink?"

"I'll have the same."

He waved to a waitress, but she looked right past him. He shrugged and pushed the bowl of peanuts toward me. "Dig in. I love peanuts, don't you?"

"Well . . ."

"Ever fly First Class on American? They warm up the nuts. That's the best. Warmed-up nuts."

I narrowed my eyes at him. Was that supposed to be like something dirty? He waved again to the waitress and this time got her attention.

He was definitely cute. Great smile, and blue eyes that were . . . I don't know . . . merry. They seemed to be seeing something funny all the time.

"Do you fly First Class often?" I asked.

"No. Never."

We both laughed.

At the far end of the bar, the sound of shattering glasses. One of the bartenders must have dropped a tray. Wild applause and laughter.

Why do people always applaud broken glass?

"Do you travel a lot?" I asked, a little hypnotized by those blue eyes.

He shrugged. "From one room to the other. I have a pretty big apartment."

The waitress brought my beer. I raised it and tilted it to his. "Cheers."

"Are you a model?" he asked.

"Excuse me?" Had he forgotten what I said in my ad?

"I know a lot of models come here. You know. These bars get a reputation as a model hangout. That's why you see all these guys in designer suits. They think that'll impress the models. And of course, it *does*."

He laughed. I didn't really think it was very funny.

"Is that why *you* come here?"

He laughed. "I came here to meet you."

I took a long sip of my beer, eyeing him the whole time. "My dad wanted me to be a model. But I never wanted to. He sent me to a modeling school when I was twelve. But I hated it. I felt . . . you know . . . awkward."

His eyes flashed. "Twelve is an awkward age."

"Colin, are you laughing at me?"

He dropped his beer bottle to the table, just barely stopped it from toppling over. "Who's Colin?"

I swallowed. "Oops. You're not Colin?"

He reached his right hand out for me to shake. "My name is Shelly Olsen. Nice to meet you . . . ?"

"Lindy Sampson. But you're the wrong guy." I turned to the bar. Now I recognized the guy at the end from his photo—Colin. He had dark hair and from this distance looked like Shelly.

"Thanks for the beer, but I made a mistake. I'm supposed to be meeting that guy over there."

Shelly held on to my hand. "But he isn't as nice as me. Look at that cruel smile. That's cold. And look how tight those jeans are. I think he's gay, Lindy. Yeah, with those jeans, he's definitely gay. You'd better stay here with me."

I laughed. "Very funny." I slid out of the booth. What a stupid mistake. Embarrassing. Well, maybe it's something for Colin and me to laugh about.

"Sorry about the mix-up, Shelly."

"No, wait. I like you. I mean . . ." He scribbled on the cocktail napkin and pushed it toward me. "My number. Call me, okay? I mean, really."

I liked him, too, I realized. He was funny and cute. Sometimes mistakes are for the good, right?

I jammed the napkin into my bag. Then I hurried to the bar.

"I'm sorry—I just can't sleep with you on our first

date!" Shelly shouted after me. People laughed. I laughed, too. Maybe I'd have a chance to pay him back someday.

"Colin, hi. I'm sorry. I made the stupidest mistake. I thought he was you!" I pointed to Shelly, who raised his bottle in a salute to us.

"Jeez," said Colin. "He does look a little like me. Why is he grinning at us like that?"

"You know, I'm not sure."

Up close, Colin didn't resemble Shelly that much. For one thing, he had a beard—or at least, his chin and cheeks were so stubbly, it looked like he'd have to shave two or three times a day. And he had that deep cleft in his chin I remembered from his photo. He was very handsome—broad forehead, strong chin. His eyes were dark brown, almost the same color as his short, wavy hair.

He wore a gray hoodie over his faded jeans, and I immediately felt overdressed again.

Maybe he saw how uncomfortable I felt because he smiled and said, "You look just like your photo, Lindy. No, much better. Would you like to go somewhere quieter and grab some dinner?"

So that's what we did. We found a Japanese place across the street and shared big platters of sushi and drank way too much sake, and talked—mainly about movies. Because Colin was really into movies, all kinds, Jackie Chan Hong Kong films, and old black-and-white films, and foreign films from all over. He told me he hangs out at the Walter Reade, the little movie theater at Lincoln Center that shows foreign films and undiscovered directors, and at the Film Forum downtown. And we talked about animation. Colin is really into animation, Japanese *anime,* new computer graphics techniques, and old Looney Tunes cartoons.

Whew! It was like taking a full-semester film course at dinner. But I loved it because I like movies, too. And it was just exciting to be around someone who cared about something so much.

Well, I liked Colin a lot. I was sorry to see the evening end. But it was two a.m. and I started to yawn. He held my arm as we stepped out to the street to find a taxi. I felt wobbly, kind of dizzy. The sidewalk seemed to tilt up and down. I leaned against him for support.

How much sake did I drink?

A lot, I guess. Because taxis went by, and we were kissing. I thought I would fall if he didn't hold me up. But he slid his arms around me and held me and I don't know how long we were standing there at the curb, kissing, my hands around his neck.

Did someone whistle at us from outside the bar across the street? I heard cars honking and another taxi rolled by. But I needed to be held, and I needed to be kissed.

Are you the guy, Colin? Are you the guy?

The question in my mind as I opened my mouth to him. Not really thinking at all, so warm from the sake and from his strong arms around me.

And then we were pressed together in the back of a taxi. I could see the black leather cap on the head of the driver as he leaned over the wheel, coffee cup in one hand, Mets game on the radio, and . . . where were we going?

Colin's apartment, all white walls and high ceilings and a tall *Casablanca* movie poster on one wall, Bogart and What's-her-name in a clinch, and another poster, all Japanese lettering and a samurai with raised sword. No time to admire the posters because I'm in his bedroom. Did he undress me or did I? My head swimming, not really trashed, but happy.

And we make love, kissing furiously the whole time. We don't know each other's bodies, but it isn't awkward. His bristly cheek brushing mine, his eyes wide as if in amazement. Yes, it feels good, even when I look up at him when it's over and wonder who he is and where I am, and how did this happen to me?

Are you the guy? Are you?

He nuzzles his scratchy face into my neck. "That was nice," he whispers.

Nice. Yeah.

He wants me to stay all night. He holds on as if he won't let me leave. But I want to go home. To think? No. To sleep.

We make a plan to meet tomorrow afternoon in the Village. He kisses my hands. So romantic.

Am I really doing this? Do I know anything about him? Does he think I'm just another Internet screw? Eye Candy. I put myself online to get laid.

Is that what he thinks?

Well, I'm all for the new technology.

He put me in a taxi and I bounced through the park to the West Side. I fumbled in my bag for money to pay the driver. And lurched out onto the sidewalk, the air warmer, almost stuffy, suddenly, or was it just me?

I wasn't tired or dizzy any longer. I felt totally wired.

Into the building. I jabbed the elevator button, eager to get upstairs and tell Ann-Marie about Colin. If she was asleep, I'd wake her up. I knew she'd be so happy I found someone I liked.

It took the car a long time to come down. The doors opened and the two gay guys from apartment six stepped out, walking Snapsy, their miniature poodle.

I said hi to Snapsy and jumped into the elevator. It's funny, I know all the dogs' names in the building, but I don't know any of the people's names. I guess that's a New York thing.

I found the apartment dark. Ann-Marie wasn't home. Probably out with Lou. And Luisa was at work.

I stepped into my bedroom and checked the phone machine. One message. I recognized the voice immediately:

"Hi, Lindy, this is Jack Smith. Listen, I had such a great time last Saturday, you know, at the play and everything. I thought maybe I'd catch you at home and we could . . . see each other maybe next week. So . . . I'll try you again and—"

I jumped, startled, when the phone rang before the message had ended. This must be Jack, trying again, I thought. Calling this early in the morning?

I really didn't want to talk to him, but the machine

was still rewinding and wouldn't pick up. So I lifted the receiver and clicked on the cordless phone. "Hello?"

I heard someone clear his throat.

"Hello? This is Lindy. Who is this?"

Then I heard hoarse breathing. Open-mouthed and slow.

"Hello? Who's there?"

No reply.

I felt a cold tingle at the back of my neck. "Hello—?"

I heard soft, slow breathing.

Someone at the other end. Someone listening to me. So close. Like being in the room with me.

A sharp intake of breath.

"Hello? Is someone there?" I didn't feel frightened, just annoyed.

More soft, steady breathing, just loud enough to be heard.

"Who's there? Who *is* this?"

No answer. A phlegmy cough in my ear.

I clicked off the phone, shaking my head. How stupid. Was that supposed to be sexy? Was it supposed to scare me? I tossed the phone onto the bed.

I kicked away my sandals and started to pull off my top. I stopped when I heard the front door open.

Footsteps in the livingroom. The front door clicked shut.

I froze.

A chill tightened the back of my neck.

First the creepy phone call, and now . . .

More footsteps, heavy thuds on the hardwood floor.

Then whoever it was bumped something, the table next to the couch, probably.

I heard a muttered curse. In a voice I didn't recognize. A cough.

Dragging footsteps now, scraping the floor.

I took a breath and finally found my voice. "Who's there? Ann-Marie? Is that you?"

10

"You totally freaked?"

"No. Not really," I said. "Well . . . just a little. I mean, you'd think crazy things, too, wouldn't you, if you had a sick phone call and then someone came creeping into the apartment?"

Colin squinted at me over the round lenses of his blue sunglasses. "And so you screamed?"

It was the next day, a sunny Sunday afternoon, the sky blue and clear as glass, the Bleecker Street sidewalks crowded with tourists window-shopping in the tiny stores and drinking espressos at little, round tables in front of cafés. Families enjoying the first nice day of spring, lots of babies in strollers and dogs eagerly tugging at their leashes, and kids on skateboards and silvery razor scooters.

"I only screamed a little," I said.

"Lindy, how do you scream only a little?"

"Like this. *Eeek.*"

We both laughed.

Holding hands, we made our way past a group of

Asian tourists trying to squeeze into a tiny boutique of Native American jewelry. A Hess oil truck making a delivery at the corner blocked the street, so traffic was backed up and not moving. Drivers honked and honked, as if that would speed up the oil delivery.

"And it was just your roommate Ann-Marie coming home?" Colin asked. "You called out, right? Why didn't she answer you?"

"Too wasted," I said. "I don't think she remembered her name."

Colin snickered. "You hungry?"

I nodded. "A quick lunch. I have to get back home. I have two manuscripts to read."

He got a pouty look on his face. Did he expect me to go back to his apartment with him and make love all afternoon?

Actually, I wouldn't mind. . . .

He looked so cute. He hadn't shaved, and his face was covered in black stubble. He had his hair brushed forward. With that cleft in his chin, he looked like a young George Clooney. He wore a loose-fitting gray sweater over faded jeans torn at one knee.

We squeezed into a tiny sandwich place on Fourth Street. "You don't look like a mortgage banker today," I said, wiping coffee stains off the menu with my napkin.

"I'm not really. I sort of do PR work. I recruit clients. You know. Go out to lunch with people. Be charming." He flashed me a phony smile.

I laughed. "You're recruiting me?"

He didn't hesitate. "Definitely."

"How did you get into that?"

He shrugged. "It's my dad's company."

I stared at him. "I see."

He raised both hands as if shielding himself. "Okay, okay. You know my guilty secret. My family is rich. So now you hate me?"

I laughed. "How do you know *I'm* not filthy rich?"

"You work in children's books."

A frazzled-looking, young waitress with pierced eyebrows and a blue heart tattoo on one side of her throat squeezed through the narrow aisle to take our order. Colin ordered a chef's salad.

"Hey, that's what I was going to order," I said.

He grinned. "See? We're totally in synch."

I rolled my eyes and ordered the chef's salad. "Now tell me your life story, Mr. Rich Guy."

Again, he didn't hesitate. I had the feeling he'd told it a lot. Grew up in quaint, quiet Greenwich, Connecticut. Had a garage band in high school. Wanted to be in a band forever, but ended up at the Wharton School of Business. Spent all his time in college going to the movies. Wanted to be a director and make commercial action films, but with style. Had a few PR jobs with productions around New York and lived off Dad. Desperately wanted money for his own apartment. Worked as a summer intern at Dad's investment firm, surprised himself by liking it and being good at it.

And girls?

It was too soon to ask him about that.

He held my hand over the table, but we didn't talk

about last night. He's going with someone, I decided, and she's away for the weekend.

Stop it, Lindy. Just enjoy the afternoon.

He had an ad on the Web site, right? Would he do that if he was involved with someone?

Maybe. Who knows?

"So, do you think your life was different?" I asked. "I mean, coming from a rich family?"

His eyes locked on mine. A strange smile crossed his face. "Well . . . I'm used to getting what I want."

An honest answer, I guess. But it made me a little uncomfortable.

And then I realized he might be talking about *me*. Am I what he wanted?

We finished lunch with espressos. I knew I should get home to my work. But I didn't want to leave him. So we made our way up Seventh Avenue, just talking and looking into store windows.

We were on our way back downtown when I felt a chill at the back of my neck. I suddenly felt uneasy.

Someone is following me, I thought. I had the strongest feeling, as if eyes were poking into my back.

I spun around, startling Colin.

Two women pushing baby strollers had the sidewalk blocked. One of them was talking rapidly on her cell phone. The other squatted down in front of her baby.

Colin raised his blue sunglasses. "Lindy, what's your problem?"

"I don't know," I said. "I just have this feeling . . ."

We turned onto Eighteenth Street. Colin wanted to pick up a book for his niece at Books of Wonder, the children's bookstore.

"You can buy her some *FurryBear* books," I said.

Colin snickered. "I don't think so. She's twelve."

He disappeared into the store.

I couldn't shake the feeling that someone was watching me. I glanced behind me again.

No, no one.

I turned to enter the bookstore—and saw Jack Smith coming toward me.

Had he been following me?

He wore a white shirt and yellow tie over black dress slacks. The tie flew up to his shoulder as he jogged up to me, waving and smiling.

"I thought that was you!" he cried.

You've been following me for blocks. And now you're acting surprised to see me?

"Jack! What are you doing here?" I tried to sound like it was a happy surprise, but I didn't quite pull it off.

"I had some business and stuff," he said. His eyes locked on mine. "What a coincidence, huh? I mean, running into you here."

"Well . . . yeah."

He pulled the tie into place, then stuffed his hands into his pockets. "Were you going into this bookstore? It's for kids, right?"

"Yeah. I—"

"It's so funny running into you. A real surprise.

Hey . . . maybe we could get a drink or something. Coffee, maybe." He nodded toward City Bakery across the street.

"Well, actually, I'm with someone."

Jack's expression changed.

Colin stepped out of the store, carrying some books wrapped in a plastic bag. I quickly took his arm and introduced him to Jack. They nodded at each other. We made awkward conversation for a few moments.

"Guess we'd better get going," I said, still holding on to Colin's arm.

"Great running into you," Jack said, flashing a half-hearted smile. "Small island, isn't it?"

Colin and I started walking to Seventh Avenue.

"Lindy, I'll call you!" Jack shouted.

At the corner, I turned and glanced back. Jack hadn't moved. He stood in front of the bookstore, staring after me.

He seemed so normal and boring.

Am I going to have a problem with him?

Well, Colin said he was used to getting what he wanted, and I guess he got it this afternoon. We ended up back at his apartment and made love, self-consciously at first, then passionately, with the bedroom windows open and sunlight streaming in, and the blanket and sheet kicked off onto the floor. . . . Sex in the daytime with someone you barely knows seems so much more decadent . . . and delicious . . . and . . . other adjectives.

What am I saying?

What am I *doing*?

No, Lindy. Dumb question. You really like him.

I didn't get back to the apartment until a little after six. Ann-Marie was in our tiny kitchen, searching for ingredients to make a sandwich. "Are you hungry?" she asked. "I'm not meeting Lou till late. I'll put this away and we can order out or something."

"I . . . don't know," I said, dropping my bag on the white Formica counter. "I—"

Ann-Marie stared at me. "Your face is all scratched up."

Colin's bristly beard.

I could feel my cheeks turning hot. I knew I was blushing.

"Where've you been? You said you were coming back at—ohmigod." Ann-Marie's mouth dropped open. She always was a good mind reader. "Lindy, I don't believe it. Who was it? That guy who took you to the comedy club? Brad?"

"No, I—" I tugged at my hair. I realized I'd forgotten to brush it before I left Colin's apartment. "Colin O'Connor," I said, avoiding her eyes. "Last night, Colin and I—"

Ann-Marie let out a scream and rushed forward to hug me. "You found someone you like? Someone you *really* like?"

"Yeah. I guess. He's very nice. He—"

She screamed again, clapping her hands. "I knew it! I knew you'd find someone. When can I meet him?

Maybe Lou and I can go out with you two next weekend."

Another hug. I'd never seen her so excited.

"No. Colin said he'll be away next weekend."

She squinted at me. "Away? He isn't married—is he?"

I laughed. "I don't think so. He has to travel for work."

"Lin, I'm so happy for you. What does he do? What's he like? Come on, spill. Tell all."

"I will," I said. "Let me just get changed. And maybe take a shower, okay? Call out. Get Chinese or something. We can sit and talk."

"Excellent." Ann-Marie opened the drawer where we keep all the restaurant take-out menus. I hurried to my room. The phone rang as soon as I entered.

I let it ring. After the weird breathing call last night, I put on the answering machine and left it on. I planned to screen my calls from now on. The machine picked up after four rings, and I heard:

"Hi, Lindy. Hope you remember me. It's Shelly. You know. The guy you met by accident. I found your number and—"

I picked up the phone and clicked it on. "Shelly? Hi. It's me. How'd you get my number?"

"Lindy, hi. You're there."

"Shelly, how'd you get my number?"

"Easy. I hacked into your computer and got all your personal info."

"No. Really."

"Really. I found it online. You know. One of those *White Pages* pages. It was totally easy. You don't expect to have any privacy these days, do you?"

"I guess not. I—"

"I don't know if you kept my number or not. I'd really like to see you. I mean, maybe we could meet by accident again. What do you think?"

I laughed. He was talking so fast, racing.

"You didn't really go out with that Colin guy, did you?" he rattled on. "I warned you about him. He's a girlie man. What was he drinking, anyway? Some kinda pink ladies' drink, wasn't it? A Cosmopolitan? Lindy, hel-lo. You don't want to go out with a guy who wears tight designer jeans and drinks Cosmos."

I thought of Colin's hand on my breasts. My cheeks burned from his rough, stubbly beard.

"Shelly, listen . . . I'm kind of busy."

"No. Don't say that, Lindy. Let's keep it simple. We'll just have coffee. Or we'll go to a dance club. Or maybe the Bahamas for a long weekend."

I laughed. "Are you trying to wear me down?"

"Yes."

"It's working."

Colin said he'd be traveling next weekend. No reason to feel guilty if I went out once with Shelly. After all, I didn't really know how Colin felt about anything. I mean, I hardly knew him.

"Okay. Saturday night," I said.

"I'm not really in the mood," he replied. And then quickly added, "Joking. Just joking. Why can't I stop joking? That sounds great, Lindy. Now, do you want to stay on the phone and get to know each other for an hour or two?"

"Bye, Shelly," I said.

"Bye."

I clicked off the phone and returned it to its base. Turning, I saw that I'd forgotten to make the bed. I make my bed every morning—one of my few habits left over from childhood.

I pulled off my top and started to slide out of my jeans when I saw the light blinking on my answering machine. A message I hadn't retrieved.

I pressed the NEW MESSAGE button and stood frozen, listening to a raspy, whispered voice . . .

"Don't say no, Lindy. Keep going out with me. DON'T EVER say no, I'm warning you. I'll mess you up—I'll REALLY mess you up if you ever say no to me."

PART TWO

11

It's a dumb joke," I said. I still felt warm from my shower. I had on a long flannel nightshirt. My wet hair was wrapped in a towel. "Come on. The food is here. Let's eat."

Ann-Marie chewed her bottom lip. "It's not a joke. It sounds serious to me."

I tore open the Chinese food bag. "Someone's idea of a sick joke."

Ann-Marie started to pace, arms crossed in front of her. "It's a threat, Lin. That raspy whisper. No way it's a joke."

I'd played the message for her. She insisted on hearing it four times.

". . . I'll mess you up!"

Ann-Marie shuddered. "Do you think it's one of the guys you just met?"

I pictured Jack, then Brad, then Colin. And Shelly? I'd just talked to Shelly. It couldn't have been Shelly. "None of them seemed like a psycho. They all seemed as normal as you and me."

"Uh-oh. You're in deep shit."

I laughed.

Should I be suspicious of Jack? Did he follow me this afternoon? I had no proof.

And Brad? I pictured that sudden, violent kiss. But he had apologized, saying he'd slipped.

"I'm just going to ignore it," I said. "I'm going to erase it. It was probably a wrong number, anyway."

"No, it wasn't. The guy said *Lindy*. He called you by name."

I began pulling out white food cartons. "Listen, do you want mustard or duck sauce?"

Ann-Marie grabbed my arm. "Lindy, you have to call the police."

"They'll tell me to ignore it."

"They won't. It's a threat. You can't just sit down and eat *moo shu* pork. You have to report a threat, Lin."

I opened the silverware drawer and pulled out chopsticks. "Well . . . I still have a friend at the Eighty-second Street precinct, remember. Tommy Foster? Ben's partner?"

"Hey, yeah. I remember Tommy. I sorta had a crush on him. Then you said he was married."

"Well, he's divorced now. I haven't really talked to him since a few weeks after Ben . . ." The words caught in my throat. Saying Tommy Foster's name was bringing back a rush of memories.

Ann-Marie picked up a rice container and began emptying it on our plates. "Think he'll be at work on a Sunday night?"

I shrugged. "Worth a try. If you insist, I'll call."

"I insist."

Ben had been such a hothead. He probably would have wanted me to start carrying a gun. Or he would have gone after all the guys I'd just met and confronted them. Tommy was older, more mature, calmer.

I'll never forget the way he sobbed at Ben's funeral. He turned away. He didn't want the other cops to see him bawl. But I saw it—and it made me cry even harder.

No one can stay dry-eyed during a police funeral. The bagpipes . . . "Danny Boy" . . . There was so much emotion in that chapel, I thought the roof would fly off.

I thought all that *feeling* might bring Ben back to life . . .

I still had the precinct phone number stored in my cell phone. I called, expecting to leave a message. But to my surprise, I was put right through to Tommy.

He sounded very surprised to hear from me. He hesitated for a long moment when I told him who it was. I guessed that my voice made him think of Ben, too.

"Working on a Sunday night?"

He snickered. "Always. I'm just taking off, actually. What can I do for you, Lindy?"

I said I had a frightening phone call I wanted to tell him about. He asked where I was living now. Practically around the corner. He said he'd stop by.

Fifteen minutes later, he showed up. Tommy is a tall, lumbering sort of guy, slump-shouldered and droopy. A Brooklyn Liam Neeson.

He was wearing a shiny, brown suit a little too big for him, a pale blue shirt and yellow tie loosened at the collar.

He looked older than I remembered, forehead creased under thinning hair, tired eyes, flecks of gray in his coppery mustache. I figured he was around forty. Why did he look so much older? Police work? Would Ben have aged so fast, too?

Would Ben have aged?

I'd have to nuke the Chinese food later. I pulled out some bottles of Corona from the fridge. The three of us chatted briefly. Ann-Marie flirted with Tommy a little. I couldn't hide my impatience. I was eager to play the phone message for Tommy and get this over.

He and I went into my bedroom. I apologized for the unmade bed. Tommy waved a hand, dismissing my apology. He stared at the answering machine as if studying it for clues.

"Let's hear it. Maybe it's a caller I recognize. There are some regulars that we get to know."

"Regular perverts?"

He shrugged. "Regular phone creeps."

I played the message for him. He shut his eyes as he listened.

"*. . . I'll REALLY mess you up if you ever say no to me!*"

The words made me shiver this time. Ann-Marie was convincing me this was serious.

Tommy scratched the back of his neck. He tilted the

bottle to his mouth and took a long sip of beer. "I don't recognize him. It's a new one. Pretty intense."

I had goose bumps on my arms. I tried to rub them away. "Think it's a joke?"

He shook his head. "No. But I don't think you should be terrified, either. There's a lot of creeps out there. You've got to be careful."

Tommy took another pull on the beer, draining the bottle, then turned his gaze back to the answering machine. "You have Caller ID?"

I shook my head. "No. You know. I was trying to save a little money."

"Did you try star-six-nine? Sometimes you can trace a call back that way."

"I was so freaked. I didn't think of it. And then someone else called. Right after I got home."

"Someone else called?"

"A guy I met last night."

He pushed the button and listened to the message again. He scratched the side of his face. "Can't place him."

"I . . . I've been dating some guys from the Internet," I stammered, feeling embarrassed. "You know. A personals Web site. They've all seemed really nice. I mean, okay. Not weird or anything."

He narrowed those tired eyes at me. "Maybe you should tell me about them."

He followed me back to the kitchen. I got him another Corona. I described my dates to him as best as I could. He listened, leaning on the kitchen counter, scribbling on a little notepad.

When I finished, he sighed. "These men might be okay. But I don't have to tell you there are a lot of geeks and freaks on the Internet."

I nodded. "And you think one of the guys I met—"

"No, maybe not. Anyone could have stolen your info, you know. Once you register at a site like that, it would be easy for anyone to access all kinds of stuff about you. Did you put your phone number on the Web site?"

"No."

"Doesn't matter, really. There are still ways they can get it. This guy doesn't even have to be in New York. He could be in Alaska or Hawaii or somewhere in Siberia."

"So I shouldn't worry?"

"You should be *careful,* Lindy. But remember this: The guys who make these phone calls, they're not killers. They're not tough guys. They're usually little creeps who live alone. The guys who make these sicko calls are all too timid and fucked-up to be dangerous."

I let out a sigh of relief. "I'll just try to forget about it then."

He scratched his neck again, then adjusted his shirt collar. "Well, you should be careful with these guys you're seeing. But I don't think there's reason to be very afraid. Keep in touch, okay? If he calls again, let me know. We'll see what we can do."

At the door, he thanked me for the beers, said it was great to see me again, told me for the tenth time not to be afraid. He hesitated for a moment. I had the feeling he wanted to say something more. But he turned abruptly, pulled the awful yellow tie tighter around his collar, and lumbered down the hall to the elevator.

"That's it!" I cried, closing and bolting the door.

Ann-Marie had just stepped into the room, carrying a copy of *In Style* magazine. "What's *it*?"

"I'm finished with these Internet dates."

"Excuse me?"

"You heard me. I don't know if one of those guys left that message or not. I just won't go out with them anymore."

She squinted at me. "Even Colin?"

I hesitated. "Well . . . I don't know. I have to think about Colin."

Are you the guy, Colin? Are you?

"But I'm through with the others. When they call, the answer is no."

In the bedroom, my phone rang.

My mouth dropped open. Ann-Marie and I stared at each other.

I strode stiffly into my room and hesitated in front of the phone. Finally, I picked it up and clicked it on. "Hello?"

"Please don't say no," a voice said.

12

Dad? Is that you? You sound funny."

"I'm on my cell. Do you believe it? I'm walking down Twelfth Street." He was shouting. He cleared his throat.

"You got a cell? Dad, you never go anywhere. Why do you need a cell?"

"Everyone has them now."

"But what are you going to do with it?"

"Talk to you, of course. I wanted to ask—"

"How's the gallbladder thing? You better?"

"It only hurts when I laugh. Ha ha. I'm fine. It's eight o'clock at night and I'm out walking around like a human."

"I can't hear you too well. You keep going in and out. What kind of phone did you get?"

"It doesn't flip. They tried to sell me one that flips. But why should a phone flip?"

"You got the cheapest one, huh? Well, why did you call?"

"Don't hang up on me. Please don't say no. I want to take you out for your birthday on Monday."

Monday?

"Dad, I completely forgot. Do you believe I completely forgot my birthday?"

Silence on his end. And I understood it.

My birthday hasn't been a happy date since I was ten. That's because it's also a horrible anniversary. The day my mother died.

And the truth is, she died *because* of my birthday.

When I turned ten, we still had the big town house duplex apartment in the Village. I don't remember that day too well. My mind is jumbled with pictures—like bright color snapshots—of red and white balloons and streamers, party hats and a pile of wrapped presents, and then . . . the crowd in the street and the cake box, the white cardboard cake box smashed, the yellow icing oozing out.

Most of what I know about that day comes from what my dad told me later, not from memory. Twelve kids were invited to the party, and my grandparents, and a magician. The Great Amazo. Why do I remember his stupid name?

Mom picked up the cake at Greenberg's bakery and was rushing home. She started across Christopher Street and didn't see the taxi. She was hit and killed half a block from the apartment. Crushed like the cake.

So you can see why I might forget my birthday. You can see why birthdays were not exactly occasions I remembered with great fondness. Dad tried to make them nice when I was a kid. He tried to be brave. And of course I had a Sweet Sixteen, all girls and giggles and loud singing and doing and redoing our hair, with the memories pushed to the background like sad music in another room.

But I could still hear it.

Dad was so busy running his chain of camera stores. I really needed a mom. Aunt Rebecca tried to step in. But it was such a chore for her, such hard work to help me with my French homework or take me shopping for summer clothes. I knew she was only doing a favor for her brother.

When the boys started coming around, I didn't know how to handle it. They told me I was beautiful. I stared at the faces of models in *Vogue* and other magazines. Was I beautiful like them?

One friend insisted I was a perfect double for Heather Graham. I looked in the mirror and couldn't see anyone but me.

In high school, I just felt too tall and gangly. My arms and legs looked so skinny to me, like broomsticks. But I was aware of people looking at me, boys watching me in the halls.

What was I supposed to do about looking the way I did?

I needed a mom to explain, to guide me through it all. I couldn't talk about it with Dad. And it was hard to talk about it with my friends.

I know, I know. I should feel lucky to be tall and blond. Ann-Marie tells me how lucky I am nearly every day.

But sometimes I just feel so awkward. Like people are judging me because . . . because I stand out.

Boo hoo, right?

Ann-Marie never lets me get away with feeling sorry for myself. And she's right.

But I feel sorry for myself on my birthday, and I have good reason. It's been fourteen years. I still dream about that smashed birthday cake oozing yellow icing onto the street. And I still miss Mom.

"Sure, I'll go out to dinner with you Monday night, Dad."

"You will?" Such surprise in his voice.

"Yeah, why not? As long as we don't talk about birthdays."

"I can't believe my little girl is twenty-four. Hear me sighing. Sigh, sigh."

"You're still young, Dad. You've got your whole life behind you."

"Oh, now you're using *my* jokes?"

"Yeah. Pretty sad, huh?"

"Well . . . I think if you . . ."

"I'm losing you, Dad. You're breaking up. You shouldn't have bought the cheap phone. Dad? Hey, Dad?"

"Oh, did *you* want coffee, too?" Rita Belson pulled the cardboard coffee container from a paper bag and set it on her desk. "Sorry. I should have asked."

"It's okay," I muttered.

We'd been working together for over a year, and I think maybe in all that time she'd brought me coffee once or twice—both times, not what I'd ordered.

Hostile?

Yes, Rita was hostile. And she didn't make much effort to cover it up.

It was three o'clock in the afternoon, and I could have used a cup of coffee. I'd spent most of the day writing letters to authors and publishers and printers, boring stuff about contracts and payments and publishing schedules.

Children's publishing is not all bunny rabbits and FurryBears, believe me.

Rita made a big deal of sifting through her stack of phone messages before sitting down at her desk to drink her coffee. She gets a lot of calls, most of them personal. She seems to have a lot of guys calling her, and she talks to them all every day.

We share a room with four gray-walled cubicles. Across from us sit Edith, a little gray-haired woman who answers the phone, and Brill, Saralynn's lanky, blond, efficient, and always fashionably dressed assistant. That means Rita and I are side by side, so I can hear every word she says on the phone.

And a lot of it is about the "great sex" she had the night before.

Whew.

Of course, when Saralynn enters the room, Rita suddenly becomes all business on the phone. She usually pretends she's discussing a manuscript with an author. I guess her many admirers understand what she's doing.

Saralynn never catches on. Rita has Saralynn totally snowed.

Rita isn't bad-looking. I can see why guys find her attractive. For one thing, she has a great body, and she shows it off well, mostly in designer stuff—TSE cashmere sweaters and scoop-necked T's; short, pleated skirts over dark stockings; a gray pinstriped Armani suit that's to die for.

She has straight, black hair down to her collar around an oval face, big blue-gray eyes, a sexy smile with one dimple in her right cheek, and a little nip of a nose, cute as a button, obviously not her original.

"Good job on this *Pioneer Girl* manuscript, Rita." Saralynn walked quickly into the room and set the stack of pages on Rita's desk. "The ending really works now."

Rita glanced at me before she turned to Saralynn. "Oh, thanks. It didn't work at all when Charlene sent it in. And the middle was a mess. I had to rewrite the whole thing. I didn't want to send it back to her again for a *third* revision, so I just stayed up all night and rewrote it myself."

"Well, it's excellent now," Saralynn said.

I had a tremendous urge to jump up and scream at her: "Don't you realize Rita says that about *every* manuscript she works on? How can it be that every single manuscript is a mess that Rita has to completely rewrite herself? She stays up all night *every time* and saves the author's work single-handedly?"

It's total bullshit, but Saralynn eats it up.

Saralynn turned to me, her smile fading. "Lindy, I need to speak to you about *Pioneer Girl II*. I read it last night. It still isn't there. You've got a great beginning and a pretty good ending—but there's no middle. Nothing happens for pages and pages. The covered wagon is stuck in a ditch and the whole story just stops."

"I know," I said lamely. "I want to talk to Charlene about it, but she doesn't answer her phone."

Charlene Nola Watson is the series author. She hates to revise. I'm sure she screens her calls and doesn't pick up when she hears it's me.

"Well, email her then," Saralynn suggested, like I'm a two-year-old who wouldn't think of email without being told. "Both of these manuscripts are supposed to go over to Random House on Friday, and only one is ready."

Rita's, of course.

Saralynn turned and swept back to her office down the hall.

Rita had a huge grin on her face. She made no attempt to hide her delight. I wanted to grab that little nub of a nose and pull it out to its original length.

"Lindy, if you'd like me to take a look at the manuscript . . . ," she sang.

Luckily, my phone rang before I could tell her what I'd like her to do with the manuscript. "FurryBear Press. This is Lindy."

"Lindy, hi. It's me."

At first I didn't recognize the voice. Was it one of the guys from the Internet?

"Just wanted to see if you've gotten any more threatening calls."

Oh. Tommy Foster.

"Tommy, I . . . didn't know you had my number at work."

"Well, I added a lot of Ben's contacts to my file. You know. In case I needed to contact some of his people. I'm just following up on last night, Lindy. If you're busy . . ."

"No. It's okay. Thanks, Tommy. I'm fine. I mean, no other calls."

"Good. I thought it might be a one-time thing. You see any of the guys you met on that Web site?"

"Well . . . I'm going out with a guy Saturday. But I didn't meet him online. And, to be honest, there's another guy . . . well . . . I kind of like him."

Tommy didn't reply. I heard someone say something to him. A police radio blared in the background. "I'd better go. You've got my number, right, Lindy?"

"Thanks, Tommy." He clicked off before I could say goodbye.

In the next cubicle, Rita was talking to one of her guys. "What are you going to wear? No, not that. No, don't wear that. Listen to me. They won't let us in if you wear that."

Where does she find all these men?

I set the phone back in its base. Nice of Tommy Foster to call. I probably shouldn't have bothered him in the first place.

I took a deep breath and let it out. It had to be someone playing a stupid joke—right?

13

"Do you like to dance?"

"Yeah. I go to clubs sometimes," I said. "You know. Downtown."

She let go of her coffee cup and reached across the table to touch my hand. "We could go dancing tonight."

"No, not tonight."

Her smile faded but her eyes were still lit up. She brushed back her long hair. It was dark brown with blond streaks in it. She put her hand over mine. "It's still early. How come you don't want to go dancing tonight?"

"I strained my back," I said.

"How?"

I snickered. "I don't want to say."

She got my meaning. She laughed. "Poor boy. I could rub it for you. I used to do massage. I'm licensed and everything."

This was starting to get interesting.

I took a real chance with this one. Her photo was so dark and out-of-focus in her ad, I thought maybe she was ugly or something. I mean, why put such a bad picture in your ad unless you're trying to hide something?

But her name was Chloe, and I'm a sucker for French names like that. At least, I think it's French. Her ad said she liked to cook, and dance, and stay out all night and be really evil, if provoked.

I remembered her ad word for word.

"Five Things You'll Find in My Bedroom: 'Happiness with four exclamation points.' "

That's pretty clever, don't you think? I mean, it got my attention.

"Music That Gets Me in the Mood: 'Music.' "

That's all it said. Just *"Music."* Ha ha. Chloe knew how to write good copy. I was getting a woody just reading her ad.

So I decided to overlook the bad photo and take a chance. She didn't turn out too bad. I mean, she's no beauty. Her face is kinda long and rectangular. And even with the blond streaks, her hair is bad news.

But she has nice eyes, very warm and inviting. And lovely, pale white skin, like a swan, and smooth as baby skin. I wanted to touch it. I could barely keep my hands away. All through dinner, I kept staring at her throat—the smooth skin just glowed.

I don't think she noticed my stare. She kept talking and laughing and reaching over to touch my hand. Yeah, she talks too much. But she has a soft, sort of whispery voice, so I didn't mind it. No matter what the fuck she's yammering about, she whispers it like she's telling you intimate secrets.

What was she talking about?

I wasn't really listening. Something about her sister. She has an audition for one of the ballet companies in town. Chloe is really jealous because she always dreamed of being a ballerina, too. But the sister has all the talent.

Maybe I should get the sister's phone number. Ha ha.

I like the little, skinny dancers who walk with their backs so straight and their toes out. Sometimes I see the ballet dancers walking in groups near Lincoln Center, probably going to class or something, and I get so hot just watching their little asses and thinking about them in their tights. And out of their tights.

I listened to what Chloe was saying about her sister. And I tried to picture the sister, a hot little thing with really powerful legs from all those ballet workouts, powerful legs that would be so good in bed. Stamina, that's what she'd have, the sister. You couldn't wear her out, I'll bet.

And I really did want to get the sister's number. I'm sure *she* didn't have to put an ad on a Web site to get guys. But how can you ask?

Besides, Chloe wasn't bad, whispering like that and touching my hand all the time, like she just couldn't wait to get to my bod.

What else did we talk about? The stock market, believe it or not.

She said she got some stocks as a present when she graduated from college. And at first, they went way up, but she didn't sell them, and now they're way down, but maybe starting to go back up, and she doesn't know what to do.

Who gives a shit?

That's what I wanted to say. But, of course, I smiled and pretended to listen, all the while staring at that beautiful, shimmery skin, that long, fine neck like a swan. Yeah, a swan. She reminded me of a fine, delicate swan. Until she stood up, that is. But that didn't happen until after dinner.

"What do you do?" she asked me, sliding a french fry into her mouth. She didn't wear lipstick or anything. Her lips were nearly as pale as her skin.

Maybe she was hoping I was a stockbroker. Then we could spend the rest of the goddamn night talking about her fucking stocks.

Okay, okay. I get a little tense when women go on and on about things I'm not into. And did she really want me—a total stranger—to tell her what she should do about her stocks?

Maybe she was just making conversation. That's what I told myself and it helped calm me down. After all, she was really sexy. I watched her sliding those french fries between her lips, and I started to feel something.

The night had a lot of promise. I like to think that every time. I know I don't sound it, but I'm a real optimist.

"So answer the question." She grinned at me. "What do you do?"

"Promotions," I said, thinking quickly. "I'm promotion director for a PR firm." Did that make any sense? I hoped so. It sounded good to me.

She tossed back her head, as if I'd said something funny.

I stared at her long, smooth neck. I wanted to sink my teeth into her throat. Like a vampire. Like a fucking vampire.

Vampires exist, you know. And maybe I'm one of them. Maybe that's what I need. To bite deep into Chloe's soft, white throat and drink. Maybe that's what I need to satisfy myself.

Nothing else works. I admit that.

Maybe that's why . . . maybe that's why . . . maybe that's why . . . what?

I can't even think straight. My brain isn't working. The cogs are jammed or something. Thinking about her throat, about drinking her blood.

Am I crazy?

Am I fucking crazy?

"What do you promote?" Chloe sips her coffee.

"Well . . . right now . . . shoes."

"Shoes?"

"Yeah. We have this shoe client. Very hot right now. Merrell. I'm doing some things with Merrell shoes."

What made me think of that? I guess because I bought a pair of Merrell shoes yesterday. They're very hip. At least, I bought them in a hip shoe store, one of those little dumpy places in SoHo where the store is about as big as a shoe box, and the sales guy, tattooed and pierced like some kind of primitive species, said they were a good choice.

"I know their shoes," Chloe says. "I've tried them on."

Like, hot shit, babe. Could we talk about stocks some more?

I pay the check. She pulls a couple of twenties from her wallet and offers to pay her half. No way. I push her hand away. She seems so grateful.

And what do *you* do, Chloe?

Did I forget to ask? Or did she tell me in that cute, whispery voice and I just forgot to listen?

We're out of the restaurant and facing Union Square Park. A steamy, damp night, a hot wind blowing newspapers and other trash around on the sidewalk. No moon or stars. They're covered by thick, low clouds.

I hold Chloe back as a bicycle delivery boy, tall bags of Chinese food in his basket, roars past. You've got to watch out for these delivery guys. They don't care if they knock you down and injure you for life. I mean, what do they care as long as they get the Chinese food where it's going, nice and hot?

"You saved my life," she jokes. She holds on to my arm.

That means this date is going to end in her apartment.

Chloe points uptown, toward the top of Union Square Park at Seventeenth Street. "Can we stop at the Barnes & Noble up there? I want to get my sister a book before her audition."

"Yeah, sure. No problem."

We cross the street into the park. Union Square has trees and walks with benches along them, but not much grass. It's mostly concrete. It used to be filled with junkies and drug dealers day and night. But they've been chased downtown and replaced by a big farmer's market where you can buy fresh-baked bread and apple cider and farm produce. Very wholesome. At night, even warm nights, the park is pretty empty.

We start to follow the path that leads uptown. Suddenly, Chloe stops and turns to me. "I'm a very direct person," she says. "I like to cut through the bullshit. You know. Cut to the chase."

"Me too," I tell her. Where is she going with this?

"Do you like me?" she asks. "Just answer point-blank. You know. Be honest."

"Do I like you? Well, yeah. I like you a lot."

She lets out a sigh and smiles at the same time. "Well, good. Because I like you, too." She brushes her face against mine, gives me a quick kiss, and takes my hand in both of hers.

Oh, Jesus. Her hands are suddenly cold and wet. Like kitchen sponges that have just finished cleaning the supper dishes.

I feel sick.

And that's when I realize she's taller than me.

I mean, how did that happen? Why didn't I notice it before? I guess because I met her at the restaurant, and she was already sitting down.

I'm really sick now. I'm totally nauseous. She's taller than me *and* holding on to me with those wet octopus hands.

My stomach heaves. I feel all my muscles tightening. My hands clench and unclench. I really can't control them.

I see her long, pale neck glowing under the streetlamp.

I glance around quickly. No one around. The park is empty, like a deserted movie set.

Her throat glows, brighter than the streetlamp. Glows as if sending out an invitation.

I didn't know she was taller than me. I didn't know her hands would be so cold and wet on my skin.

Is this the night I become a vampire? Can I do it? Can I sink my teeth into the beautiful, throbbing, shimmery throat?

No. I'm too frightened.

I raise my hands to the sides of her neck. She smiles at me. What is she expecting? Tenderness?

Can't she see how sick I am? Can't she see me struggling to keep my dinner down? She has fucked up everything. It isn't my fault. I tried, didn't I? I really tried.

I wrap my hands around her neck. I can feel the blood pulsing in her throat. My hands are on their own now. I'm too sick to control them.

She whispers my name.

Whispers my name so sweetly.

I can't take this. How am I supposed to deal with that?

My hands slide off her neck. I spin away from her. The white globes of the streetlamps dance in front of me. The lights leap and bounce in a frantic ballet.

I hear her voice, hear her calling to me.

She sounds far behind me now. Because I am running. Running out of the park. Running into the darting, dancing lights.

I tried so hard.

Why didn't I get her sister's name? And her number?

Chloe's sister would be small, petite, with tiny, dry hands, dry as the powder they put on their ballet slippers.

No, don't be sick on the street. It's over. It's time to start again.

I run all the way to my apartment. People stare at me, but I don't care. I can't wait to get online. I can't wait to see the faces of the girls staring out at me on the screen so expectantly, so sweetly.

"Be cool. Be cool," I tell myself, breathing hard. I can't control my breathing. My hand shakes the mouse. I scroll down quickly from face to face.

"Be cool. Just be cool."

But the women . . . they drive me crazy.

14

I like to make lists. They make me feel as if I'm organized. Sometimes I make lists just to kill time. . . . Friends I'd invite to my birthday party if I was having one, clothes I'd like to buy this fall if I could afford them, books I'd like to read . . .

Tommy Foster told me to forget about the threatening phone call, but I couldn't. One night after work, I sat down at the little desk in my room, took out a pad of paper, and started to write a list.

Maybe if I wrote down what I knew about the guys I recently met, something would click. Something would tell me who the caller was.

Also, I knew that if I got it all down on paper, I could stop running it over and over again in my mind. Had I been able to think of anything else? Not much. I think even Saralynn had begun to notice how distracted I was.

Luisa was in her room getting ready for work. I could hear her radio blasting Hot97. Luisa is really into hip-hop and rap—has been ever since she met Dr. Dre at a party.

I admit I went through a short Eminem period, and there's a new Outkast single I really like. But I'd much rather dance to that music than listen to it.

In the livingroom, Ann-Marie was arguing loudly on the phone with Lou. Trouble in paradise? No. It didn't sound like a major battle. Some mix-up in plans.

I closed my bedroom door, settled down at the desk, and forced myself to shut out everything else and concentrate on my list.

First I wrote down the names of the guys in the order I'd met them: Brad, Jack, Shelly, Colin. I left plenty of space under each name. Then I tried to write down everything I remembered—not about their looks, but about their lives and the way they acted. Anything that might help me figure out which one had threatened me.

BRAD FISHER

1. Took me to a noisy restaurant, then to a comedy club.
2. Not much conversation.
3. Smoked a lot, drank a lot of beer, but it didn't seem to affect him.
4. A real New Yorker, grew up near Coney Island.
5. Writes for a weekly newspaper; very ambitious.
6. At comedy club, laughed hardest at jokes that were insulting to women. Laughed and clapped at all the antifemale remarks and put-downs. (IS THIS IMPORTANT? DOES THIS TELL ME

SOMETHING ABOUT BRAD? OR AM I MAK-
ING TOO MUCH OF IT? EVERYONE ELSE
WAS LAUGHING, TOO.)

7. Grabbed me and forced me to kiss him really hard
at end of date. I felt like he was being violent. Or
did he slip from the taxi? Maybe just an awkward
moment?

8. Seemed okay till that last moment. Maybe too
many beers explains it. (DOES HE DRINK TOO
MUCH AND GET VIOLENT? OR AM I TO-
TALLY WRONG ABOUT THIS?)

JACK SMITH

1. Boring as hell. Talks mainly about his work,
which is also boring as hell. Does this mean he's
repressed?

2. Cheap. Date was a total freebie.

3. Became emotional, had tears in his eyes over
sucky patriotic musical. Further sign of repressed
feelings? Does bland exterior hide an unbalanced
mind?

4. Emails every day and phoned four or five times
even though I discouraged him. (Only one of the
four guys to call so often.)

5. Ran into me in the Village and pretended it was a
coincidence. (Was it really a coincidence? Why did
I have a strong feeling he'd been following me?)

SHELLY OLSEN

1. Seems sweet. Very baby-faced and cute-looking. Haven't been out with him yet. Only met him for a few minutes. (By mistake.)
2. He's funny. Good sense of humor.
3. Eager to see me. Eager enough to track down my phone number on the Internet.
4. Called soon after the threatening phone call. IS THAT A COINCIDENCE?
5. Seems unlikely he'd say, "Keep saying yes to me," in a threatening phone message since I hadn't yet said yes to him. SHOULD I CROSS HIM OFF THE LIST?

COLIN O'CONNOR

1. We hit it off right away. Just seemed to click.
2. I liked his passion for movies. He could get really stoked just talking about films he liked. DOES THAT MEAN HE GETS OBSESSED ABOUT OTHER THINGS, TOO?
3. I liked his passion for ME.
4. Is he obsessed with me??

I couldn't write anything more about Colin. I felt totally mixed up about him, because . . .
Because . . .

I wasn't ready to face what I was thinking—the dread that had kept me awake nights.

I set the pen aside and scanned the list. Lindy, you should have been a psych major.

Well, I did take two psych courses at NYU. I think I got B's in both. I was your solid B student without having to work hard. Even with two majors, I didn't work hard in college. It was easier than Stuyvesant High. I read a lot, got high with Ann-Marie and my other roommates, and worried about my so-called social life.

We all went out a lot. To movies and dance clubs and museums and concerts in the park. There's a lot to do in New York City. It's not like going to college anywhere else. It's the City That Never Sleeps, you know. So we seldom slept.

Yes, yes. Simpler times.

Hey, I'm only twenty-four. How can I be nostalgic *already*?

Twisting a strand of hair around one finger, I held the list up close to the lamp. I read it over one more time, trying to find some clue . . . any clue.

Trying to ignore the one thought I hadn't written on the list. The one thought that kept me shuddering at night, even with the blankets pulled up over my chin.

Colin.

The whispered voice on the tape. The last few times I listened to it, I thought I recognized him. Recognized the voice.

Colin.

15

Where are you going?" Ann-Marie appeared at my bedroom door. She was chewing on one of those energy bars with about twice as many calories as a Snickers bar. She eats about five of them a day. She thinks they're okay because she buys them in a health food store.

"Out," I replied, fixing my hair in the mirror. I was trying out a new lipstick color. Bubblegum pink. Kind of kicky.

"Who with?" Ann-Marie stepped into the room and sat down on the edge of my bed.

"A guy."

I pulled a white, Triple 5 Soul baseball cap down over my hair and scrunched the bill down on the sides. Cute.

Luisa stepped up beside the bed. "You're going out with one of those Internet guys, aren't you."

I turned to her. "No, I'm not. *Mom*."

Luisa raised both hands, like for a truce. "Whoa. We're not in a bitchy mood tonight, *are we*?"

"Sorry," I said. "Maybe I'm a little stressed. I don't know."

"So you *are* going out with one of those guys," Ann-Marie accused. She finished the energy bar and crumpled the wrapper in her hand.

"Why do you eat those things? Do you really think they give you energy?"

She tossed the wrapper at me. "Sure, if I drink a lot of coffee with them. Don't change the subject, Lindy."

"I like your hat," Luisa said. "Where'd you get the T-shirt?"

"Banana Republic, I think. It's pretty old."

"It matches your lipstick."

"I'm not sure about the lipstick," I said, turning back to the mirror. "Too teeny-bopper. Shelly is going to take me out for a milkshake and a pony ride."

Ann-Marie narrowed her eyes at me. "Shelly, huh?"

"Which one is he?" Luisa asked.

"The one I *didn't* meet on the Internet," I said.

Ann-Marie picked up one of my hair scrunchies and twisted it around in her hands. "He's the one you met by accident."

"Yeah. A lucky accident," I said. "He's nice. Sweet. Baby-faced."

"Baby-faced." Ann-Marie snickered. "What makes you think Baby Face is okay?"

I shrugged. "Just a hunch." I turned to her. "Hey, don't worry, okay? It's just dinner."

"Have any of those other guys called?" Luisa asked.

"Well . . . Brad emailed me."

"He's the reporter?"

"Yeah. He wanted to take me to Belmont to watch horse races. And of course Jack emailed and called."

"The freebie guy."

"Yeah. He keeps trying. I haven't called him back once. But he doesn't give up."

Ann-Marie slid the scrunchie around her wrist and twirled it. "Is he, like, a stalker? Think he's the one who made that creepy call?"

I shrugged. "I don't think so."

"So what did you tell these guys?" Luisa asked.

"I told them I was busy, that's all."

"You'll just keep telling them you're busy till they get the idea?"

"That's the plan."

Luisa fiddled with one of her dangling red earrings. "But Shelly is okay?"

I jumped up and headed to the door. "I'll let you know after tonight."

16

Shelly was waiting for me in the lobby downstairs. He wore faded jeans and a pale blue Polo shirt under a blue blazer. He flashed me a warm smile as I stepped out of the elevator.

"Hi," I said. "Are you Shelly? Am I sure you're the right guy?"

His eyes flashed. "You've got the right guy this time," he said.

I followed him out the door. It was muggy out, hot with a wet wind blowing. "Where are we going?" I grabbed my cap in time to stop a gust of wind from lifting it off my head.

"How was that Colin guy?" he asked, grinning at me. "Gay, right? I knew I had his number."

I laughed. "No. He was nice. Stop talking about him."

"Nice, but gay. Not that there's anything wrong with that."

We both laughed. I guess he watches *Seinfeld* reruns, too. I took his arm. "Where are you taking me?"

He stared at me. "I thought *you* were taking *me*!

Didn't you promise me dinner at The Four Seasons and then a show?"

I squeezed his shoulder. "You're very funny tonight."

"Funny-looking?"

"No. I like the way you look," I said. "Sort of a dark-haired Huck Finn in yuppie clothes."

He pretended to be offended. "I look like a hick?"

"Yeah." I laughed.

Now he looked *really* offended.

"I'm joking."

"I hate women with a sense of humor."

"I'll remember that," I said.

We were walking east on Seventy-ninth Street. When we came to the Museum of Natural History, we turned uptown, then continued east on Eighty-first. The museum, a pale-brick, gothic-like structure, turrets and all, stretches for blocks. Someone told me it's in the *Guinness Book*—the biggest museum in the world.

We walked past the newly built planetarium. The giant sphere inside the Rose Observatory sent its blue glow out into the night. Very romantic. But I was hungry, and we seemed to be walking *away* from all the restaurants.

It was a little after eight-thirty. The museum was closed, but several people—couples mostly—sat on the front steps, talking, smoking, hanging out.

A bus rolled by, then Shelly pulled me across Central Park West. "Lindy, I hope you're into gourmet food."

"Excuse me?" I glanced around. "Where are we going? Into the park?"

I felt a sudden stab of fear. This part of the park would be deserted this time of night. I pictured Shelly dragging me into the playground . . . forcing me to the ground . . . *forcing* me.

God, how awful. I came out for a nice time, a pleasant evening, and here I was thinking the most horrible things. It's so frightening how one call, one thirty-second phone message, can change the way you think.

Did he notice my fear? It was too dark here. He couldn't see my face.

He grabbed my arm firmly. I glanced up and saw that his eyes were narrowed, his features set.

He pulled me toward the park entrance. I didn't see anyone around, except for a hot dog vendor, bending over his cart, his back turned.

My throat tightened. I tried to pull free of his grasp.

Why didn't Shelly speak? Why didn't he say anything?

He *was* dragging me into the park!

17

Shelly? What are we doing? Where are we going?" My voice came out high and shrill.

"Here we are." He let go of my arm.

The hot dog vendor turned. He was a short, dark-haired man in a stained white apron. He smiled when he saw Shelly. "Mr. Shelly, here you are. *Buenas noches, señor.*"

My heartbeat began to slow to normal. I whispered to Shelly, "He knows you?"

"I made a reservation," Shelly said. "Sometimes it gets very crowded." Then he introduced us. The hot dog guy's name was Paulo. *"Qué bonita,"* he said, eyeing me up and down.

"What's good tonight?" Shelly asked him. "Hot dogs?"

"I'm just closing up shop, Mr. Shelly," Paulo said. "When the museum closes, I close, too." He stared up at me and smiled. "But I saved a few of the best for you. What do you want on them? Everything?"

"Four with everything," Shelly said before I could answer.

Paulo opened the lid on his cart and began fishing around in the boiling water. I pulled Shelly to the front of the cart. "Gourmet food, huh?"

"They're the best dogs in New York," he said seriously. "I don't know what he does to them, but trust me."

"Very cute," I said.

"What's cute?"

"This whole thing. Buying me hot dogs. Being on a first-name basis with the cart guy. Very cute. I feel like I'm in a Reese Witherspoon movie."

"You're cute, too," he replied. "Everyone's cute tonight."

I laughed. I felt terribly relieved. And angry at myself for thinking such sick thoughts about Shelly.

We sat down on a park bench across from the museum, ate the hot dogs, and shared a can of Yoo-Hoo. I finished the first dog and half of the second. That was all I could manage, especially since they were loaded down with chili and relish and sauerkraut and mustard. Shelly forced me to agree they were the best hot dogs in New York. Actually, they were a real treat. I don't eat hot dogs very often—a girl has to watch her calories, right?

Shelly finished my leftover half. "Can't let dogs like these go to waste."

"Shelly, I've never met anyone so intense about hot dogs."

He didn't smile. "I'm intense about everything. I'm a real intense guy. It's just . . . me."

"You know, I don't know anything about you," I said. "Where do you live? What do you do?"

"Want my social security number?"

I laughed. "Yes, and two forms of ID."

He waved to Paulo, who began rolling his cart down the middle of Central Park West. "I have an apartment across the street," he said. "Just a studio, but it's not too small. It has an extra little room where I can work."

"You work at home?"

He crunched the Yoo-Hoo can in his hand. "Yeah."

"What do you do?" This was like pulling teeth. Why didn't he just tell me?

He stared across the street at the museum. "I'm a writer."

I laughed. "You sound so ashamed."

Again he didn't smile. "I don't like to talk about it much. I mean, if I was a *published* writer, I could talk about what I'd published. But since I'm not . . ."

"What do you write?" I persisted. "If you write picture books, I could help you. I work at a children's publisher."

He tossed the soda can toward the mesh trash basket on the corner. He missed and the can rolled onto the sidewalk. "I write . . . fiction," he said finally. "Short pieces, actually."

"You mean short stories?"

"Yeah. Kinda. Slice-of-life type stuff. Pieces."

"Literary stuff?" I asked. "Shelly, are you a secret intellectual?"

He snickered. "What does that mean? *Secret intellectual?* Were you an English major or something?"

That made me grin. "Actually, I was. And, I had a second major in business. It looked good on my résumé when I was applying for publishing jobs."

"I don't have a résumé," he muttered, still avoiding my eyes. "But I really enjoy writing. It's the only time I feel . . . powerful."

Whoa. This was getting a little heavy. Wasn't this just supposed to be a starter conversation? I could feel my cheeks turn hot.

"So you're not published yet? I don't mean to get too personal, but how can you afford an apartment on Central Park West? Do you have another job?"

He shook his head. "Good old Mom bought it for me."

"Nice," I said. "She supports your writing?"

He stared across the street. "She hasn't seen any of it yet."

Time to change the subject, Lindy. "Where are we going next?" I asked. I started to stand up.

"Do you write?" he asked at the same time. "I mean, at your job."

"Not really. I do a lot of *re*-writing. I think editing is fun. But it's a whole different thing from writing."

"What made you decide to go into publishing?" he asked.

I shrugged. "Beats me. It was something I thought about even in high school. I've always enjoyed hiding behind a good book, I guess."

His eyes flashed. "Hiding?"

I could feel my cheeks burning again. "Well, yeah. Hiding. My dad . . . he was always pushing me to be a model or an actress or something like that. He wanted me to use my looks. He said I could make a fortune."

Shelly wiped chili off his chin. "But you didn't buy it?"

"No way. I mean, I didn't really think I was . . . so great-looking. I thought he was just being a dad. You know, thinking I was prettier than I was. Modeling classes. Acting classes. I just felt I didn't belong. And so I used to hide behind a book. I was always at the library. I always had my face in a book."

Shelly studied me for a long moment in silence. I couldn't read his expression.

"I'm sorry," I said, jumping to my feet. "I don't know where that came from. I didn't mean to lay that all on you."

"And did you feel guilty?" he asked, his blue eyes locked on mine.

"Excuse me?"

He continued to stare. His expression was intense, needy somehow. "Did you feel guilty? Did you feel guilty for letting your father down?"

Guilty? Change the subject, Lindy. This is getting weird.

"I never thought about that," I said. I turned away. I couldn't stand that penetrating stare. What did he want? Why was he asking that? Just trying to understand?

"Thanks for giving me something new to worry about!"

It was a joke, but he didn't even smile. "It's not good to feel guilty," he said softly. "I know where you're coming from."

I grabbed his hands and pulled him to his feet. "Enough about that, Shelly. We've had an awesome gourmet dinner. Now what do you want to do?"

I took him to Whale, the dance club downtown where Ann-Marie and Lou hang out. After all that talk, I felt like dancing. And I wanted Ann-Marie to check him out.

Why did I open up to Shelly that way? Because he seemed nice and smart and I wanted to see if he was understanding, too? Because of that boyish, open face that seemed so trustworthy?

Or was I lonelier than I knew?

I could always tell my deepest thoughts to Ben. After he died, there really wasn't anyone I could confide in. Of course, Ann-Marie is a good, close friend. But she is the one who confides in me, not the other way around. It's just the way our relationship is. You know how it works. Everyone has her role.

Whale was an old warehouse in the meat-packing district that had been converted to a dance club. It was a huge, high-ceilinged, windowless square room with balconies running along all four walls. The platform for the dj and all his equipment were plopped right in the middle of the dance floor. A long, red velvet bar and a row of low tables stretched along the back wall.

The décor was all red and gold. A red neon sign with WHALE in a fancy script was suspended from the ceiling over the dj's platform. There were no whales on the walls or ceiling balcony sides. No sea colors. No splashing waves. No photos of whales leaping out of the ocean. This was not a theme place.

Ann-Marie had told me that the club owner's nickname was Whale. She said he was a huge, blubbery guy—maybe four hundred pounds—who showed up mostly on weekends wearing enormous red and gold pajamas, and danced his guts out, taking up most of the dance floor.

She said he was a real sleazy letch, always trashed, usually coked out of his gourd, who liked to trap girls against the wall with his big belly and feel them up.

Nice.

Why do Ann-Marie and Lou like this club? Lou and Whale went to the same high school in Larchmont—before Whale dropped out—so they get in free, and sometimes Whale comps them on the drinks.

Anyway, there was no sign of Whale tonight, which helped the party atmosphere a *lot*. The dance floor was jammed and people were three-deep at the bar. I pulled Shelly through the crowd until I found Ann-Marie and Lou standing at a table near the bar, tall beer glasses in their hands.

Ann-Marie looked awesome. She wore a tight, short black skirt and a shiny orange top that left about two inches of stomach showing. Very sexy.

She mopped her forehead with a cocktail napkin. Her hair glistened with sweat. "Hey!" she raised her glass and smiled as Shelly and I approached.

"You've been dancing!" I had to shout over the throbbing beat of the music and the roar of voices.

She leaned close and shouted in my ear. "I twisted my ankle. We had to stop." She tilted the beer glass to her mouth and gulped it all down. "Got to replenish."

I introduced Shelly. Lou went to the bar to get more beers. Ann-Marie talked about how lucky it was that Whale hadn't showed up tonight. "He makes the dj play Cher over and over."

Shelly leaned over the table and grinned at Ann-Marie and me. "I love clubs like this. I think I'm really going to get my freak on tonight!"

Get his freak on? He was joking, right? Where did he get that line—VH1?

Ann-Marie laughed. "This guy's cute," she whispered in my ear.

Lou was returning with the beers, but Shelly pulled me away from the table, onto the dance floor. I bumped a girl with a tattoo of a grinning monkey on her shoulder. She turned away, her tight silver pants reflecting the bouncing lights, blond hair flying, and I glimpsed another monkey face on her other shoulder.

Shelly and I found a space near the side of the dj's

platform and started to dance. After a few seconds, I realized that Shelly was a fabulous dancer.

He had his eyes closed. His arms were sliding gracefully up and down. His knees were bent and his hips were bumping and swaying in perfect rhythm to the music.

I tried to keep up with him, get in rhythm with him. But he was really good and totally into it.

The beat changed as the dj mixed in a new song. I tried to pull Shelly back to the table, but he kept on dancing. He put his hands on my waist and guided me. He didn't want to stop.

When the dj mixed in a new track, Shelly opened his eyes. He took my hand. He had a sweet smile on his face. He leaned close. "Told you I was intense." He was breathing hard. He seemed very pleased with himself.

I pulled him back to the table. He picked up his beer and drained it. He lowered the glass, still breathing hard. He made no attempt to wipe the foam off his mouth.

I laughed. "You look like a rabid dog." I picked up a cocktail napkin and wiped the foam off his mouth and chin.

Lou had his arm around Ann-Marie's waist. "Hey, you're a good dancer," he told Shelly.

Shelly's dark hair fell over his forehead. "Thanks. I've just always been into music."

Ann-Marie brought her face close to mine and whispered. "Jesus. Think he's like that in bed?"

I slapped her hand. "Shut up."

"If he is, he's a keeper!"

"No, really. Shut up."

She laughed.

We all chatted for a while. And danced some more. And I finally started to relax and have a good time.

After a while, we'd danced so hard my legs were trembling. Ann-Marie and I made our way to the ladies' room. "Shelly seems sweet," she said. "Like him?"

"I haven't decided," I said. "He's cute enough and very funny. But then sometimes he's kind of . . . disturbing."

When we returned, Lou and Shelly were watching a platinum blonde with enormous boobs dancing in what appeared to be a tiny, blue bikini top over matching blue short-shorts. The two guys were practically drooling.

"What do you think she does during the day?" Ann-Marie asked me.

"Supreme Court justice?"

Ann-Marie grabbed the sides of Lou's head and turned it away from the platinum blonde. "Time to go."

We said our goodbyes and nice-to-meet-yous. Ann-Marie led Lou across the dance floor.

Shelly was still staring at the bouncing blonde.

"Do you want to go, too?" I asked, shouting over the beat, beat, beat.

He finished his beer. "No way. It's still early." He took my hand and led me back onto the dance floor. We danced a long time, drank a few beers, then danced some more.

When we finally stepped out of the club, it was

nearly two in the morning. A cold spring rain poured down hard. West Twelfth Street was shiny with water running in the curbs like rivers. Rain pattered the tin roofs of the meat-market warehouses.

"It must have been raining a long time," I said, grabbing his arm. "Maybe we can get a cab on Tenth."

Shelly laughed and raised his face to the rain. "Cab? Why do we need a cab?" He pulled me onto the sidewalk.

"We don't have umbrellas. I don't have a raincoat or anything," I complained. "What do you think you're doing?"

A taxi rolled up to the restaurant across the street, and a couple climbed into it.

Shelly pulled off his blazer and wrapped it around my shoulders. "Don't you love rain? It's so fresh and . . . and . . . wet."

How many beers did he drink? I wasn't counting, but . . .

"Shelly, we're getting drenched! Let's jog to Tenth and find a cab."

"But, Lindy, doesn't the rain make you want to sing?"

"Sing? Hel-lo. We're drowning here."

He began belting out "Singing in the Rain" at the top of his lungs.

I heard laughter and saw a couple under a black umbrella, arms around each other, laughing as they hurried past.

How lame is this? I thought, watching him do a splashy tap dance as he sang.

Sorry, Shelly. You're pushing it with the Gene Kelly act.

"Hey, don't you like that song?" Shelly asked, grabbing my arm. Water soaked through his shirt. His hair was matted to his forehead.

"No way!" Laughing, I pulled him down the block, his blazer over my head.

A taxi appeared at the corner, windshield wipers sending up a spray of water. It had its OFF-DUTY sign lit, but the driver pulled over and asked where we were going. When I told him Seventy-ninth and Amsterdam, he said, "Jump in."

I climbed in and slid across the seat. Shelly stood at the car door, shaking water off like a dog. Then he lowered himself into the cab. The driver grumbled something. I couldn't hear him through the Plexiglas divider. The taxi took off, wheels whirring on the rain-slicked street.

Breathing hard, raindrops clinging to his dark eyebrows, running down his cheeks, Shelly pretended to pout. "I didn't get to finish the song." He hummed a few more bars.

"You're totally crazy," I said.

He wiped water from his forehead. "Yeah. Tell me something I don't know."

"You look normal, but you're not," I teased.

"Sometimes I lose it a little," he said solemnly, lowering his eyes. "Therapy doesn't help. I'm thinking of joining an Ashram."

"Really?"

"No."

I leaned close and kissed his cheek. It felt cold and wet, like a fish.

He turned and pressed his lips against mine. A nice kiss.

"Can I read your writing sometime?" I asked.

"No," he answered sharply.

18

Shelly was fun to be with. But he seemed to switch personalities in seconds. He had been so thoughtful when we were talking on the park bench. And then at the club he'd become a different person.

Was I being too analytical?

Was he just a thoughtful guy who also liked to have fun?

Maybe I needed someone like Shelly to draw me out, to help me be less self-conscious.

The elevator stopped on the eleventh floor. I was home. I stepped out into the long, green-carpeted hall. No one around this time of night, but as I passed by I could hear loud music from apartment 11-C and angry, arguing voices from 11-D across the hall.

Our apartment, 11-J, is at the very end of the hall. The corner is dark because the bulb is out in the last ceiling fixture. We've complained to the super about it for weeks, but so far, no fresh bulb.

I fumbled around in my bag, trying to find my key in the dark—when the door swung open and Lou stepped out. Startled, we both let out short cries. Lou lurched into me. I felt as if I'd been bumped by a truck.

"Oh. S-Sorry," he stammered. His *s*'s whistled.

I backed into the corner. "Lou. Hi. You're still here?" Duh.

He grinned at me, a lopsided grin. Even in the dark, I could see that his eyes were glassy. He was breathing hard, his big chest heaving up and down. His furry eyebrows folded as he struggled to focus on me.

"Lindy . . ."

"Lou, back up. Are you totally trashed?"

"Lindy, listen—" He shut his eyes. His sour breath made me cringe.

"Hel-lo. Lou, you've got me cornered here. Back up a little, okay?"

He didn't move. Instead, he shot both arms out, blocking my escape. He smelled of sweat and beer and stale pot smoke. "I want to tell you . . ." He opened his eyes. He gazed at my breasts, then slowly raised his eyes to my face. "Lindy . . ."

"Lou, we'll have a nice chat some other time, okay? Can I help you downstairs? Let me get you a taxi."

"I want to tell you . . . you're so awesome-looking."

"Thanks, Lou. But I've been dancing for hours. I'm kind of wiped. Could you let me—"

"You're so fucking bootiful, Lindy." He let out a giggle, as if he'd said something funny.

I tried to squeeze around him, but he moved quickly to block my path. "Lou, I don't like this game. Let me go. I mean it."

"So fucking bootiful."

"You can hardly speak. Please, give me a break here. Just take a step back. You know what? Come back inside the apartment. You shouldn't go home like this."

My heart started to pound. He was like a bear, and I was cornered. He blinked at me and giggled again.

"Let's go inside, okay?"

"Bootiful." Instead of backing up, he grabbed my waist with both hands and pressed his face against mine. His cheek felt burning hot, and moist.

I felt panic sweep over me.

I can't breathe. He's going to suffocate me.

"So bootiful . . ."

"Lou, get off me. Now! I mean it. Get *off*!"

He wrapped his arms around me, pressing me against the wall. His wet lips brushed my ear. He lowered his hands to my breasts and started pawing them roughly. "Do you have any idea how fucking awessssome you are?"

Should I stomp on his foot? Should I kick him in the balls? I don't want to injure him. I just want to get him off me.

Should I call for help?

"Get *off*! Get your hands *off* me!"

Finally he let go of my breasts. He lifted his face from mine and squinted at me. "Do you know why I stay with Ann-Marie?" Sweat ran down his forehead, his cheeks.

"I . . . don't want to hear this. Please. You crossed a line here, Lou. You're really scaring me."

"Just to be close to you, that's why."

"Stop it, Lou. Just shut up, okay? I'm going to—"

"Tha'ssss why I stay with her." Another insane giggle. "I think about you all the time."

"Shut up, Lou." I didn't mean to shout, but I couldn't help it.

What is he planning to do? Is he going to grab me again?

No, no. Take a breath. He's out of his head. You can't afford to panic. You have to be the calm one.

"Really. No shit, Lindy. All the time I'm with her, I'm thinking about you."

"Please please please. Listen to me, okay?" I brought my arms up fast and shoved him hard.

Startled, he toppled back into the apartment door. He hit it so hard, I thought he might break the door.

But here was my chance. I scrambled around him, away from the wall. My legs were trembling. My whole body shuddered. But I was in the clear. I hoped.

"I feel so close to you. I want to be with you. You're so bootiful."

I rubbed my cheek. It was still wet from his sweat. "Let's get you a taxi. I promise I won't tell Ann-Marie. Just stay away from me. Be a good boy, Lou, and I promise I won't tell Ann-Marie."

"Do you like me, Lindy?" He suddenly had this little-boy expression, his glassy eyes all wide and hopeful. "Do you like me?"

"I like you, Lou. But let's get you home, okay? I won't tell Ann-Marie. I promise."

He nodded. "Good." He wiped the sweat off his face and forehead with his shirt sleeve. "Good. It will be our sssecret, right? Our little secret?" He eyed my breasts again.

I started toward the elevators at the other end of the hall. I suddenly felt weary, as if he'd drained all my strength away. I turned and made sure he was following me.

His shoulder dragged against the wall as he walked. "Our little secret. You're so totally awesome. Do you know that, Lindy? You don't mind, do you? Ha ha. You don't mind if I call you, Lindy? I mean—if I . . ."

"Shhh. Take it easy. You'll be fine. You just had a little too much—"

He pulled a clear plastic envelope from his shirt pocket and waved it in front of my face. I saw white powder inside. "Want some?"

"No, please. Put it back."

He pushed his bottom lip out in a pout. He suddenly looked like a big baby.

"Put it away, Lou."

He obediently stuffed it back in his pocket. "I never get high," he said, shaking his head. "Isn't that a shame? I never get high."

"You're doing a pretty good imitation," I said. I was breathing normally now, no longer trembling, over my fear. As we passed, I heard the couple still arguing in 11-D. I felt grateful no one had heard Lou and me out in the hall.

I pushed the elevator button. I couldn't wait to get

rid of him. And what would I find in the apartment? Ann-Marie passed out on the couch? Or totally high, chattering away, demanding to stay up all night and bond?

"Just can't get high," Lou muttered, pressing his forehead against the elevator door. "No matter what. It's weird, isn't it? Fucking weird."

I tugged him back just as the door slid open. Then I took him by the hand and led him into the elevator. When the door closed, I had another moment of panic.

Will he come on to me again? Will he try to smother me again? He has me trapped here.

But no. He leaned on the metal rail with his head tilted back against the elevator wall, eyes closed, a smile on his face, humming to himself. When the car bounced to a stop on the first floor, Lou bounced with it, his knees buckling, legs nearly collapsing under him.

He giggled. "Are you hungry?"

"No. Come on." I pulled him to the front door.

"Want to get a burger or something?"

"No. I'm really not hungry."

"Pizza? Just a slice?"

Out onto Seventy-ninth Street. The rain had slowed to a steady drizzle. Light from the streetlamps shimmered in the wet street. Two men with black umbrellas stood waiting for the crosstown bus at the corner. The newsstand there was dark and closed up.

I stepped into the street to get Lou a taxi. He bumped up against my side. "I get so hungry when I'm loaded. Ha ha."

I saw a taxi with its light lit at the end of the block and started to wave frantically.

"But I can't get high. It's the weirdest thing. Do you like me? I mean, really like me? Ha ha."

"Oh, thank goodness," I said as the taxi pulled up beside us. I opened the door and shoved Lou into the back. He hit his head on the Plexiglas divider, let out a groan, then settled back in the seat.

"Our little secret," he said, grinning.

"Bye, Lou." I slammed the car door and watched gratefully as the taxi roared away.

As the elevator carried me back up to the eleventh floor, I felt as if I were being transported through a different world. Lou's gross behavior in the hall had changed everything. Shifted reality in an ugly way.

I felt as if I'd been in some sci-fi moment where you find yourself in a parallel universe—your surroundings look exactly the same, but the people you know act differently, not at all like themselves, and everything you thought true wasn't true anymore.

Was he telling the truth about how he felt about me? Did he really stay with Ann-Marie to be close to me?

No. I couldn't believe that. No way I wanted to believe it.

I held my stomach. I suddenly felt sick.

Wait. He was coked out of his head. He could barely speak. Why should I take anything he said seriously?

I should shut it out of my mind. He won't remember a thing tomorrow.

But . . . he'd *mauled* me. He'd forced me against the wall. He'd pressed his face, his body against mine. He'd played with my breasts. He'd mauled me like a bear.

He is dangerous.

Don't get carried away. You don't want to tell Ann-Marie about this. No way. Ann-Marie is totally crazy about him. She acts so jealous when anyone else comes near him.

You can't tell her.

But what if it's true? What if he's a total pig who's just using her?

No. I can't tell her. She'll hate me forever. I'll lose my best friend.

My bag. Where is my bag?

I raised both arms, expecting to see it on one of them. But no. Did Lou take my bag? Of course not.

The elevator bounced to a stop. I lurched out before the door was fully open. Then I ran down the hall, my shoes thudding on the carpet. Yes, there it was in the corner. It must have fallen from my hands when Lou came out of the apartment.

I picked it up off the floor, rummaged around in it till I found my key. I opened the door slowly and poked my head in, expecting to find Ann-Marie in the livingroom.

No. The lamp beside the couch was on dim. No one on the couch. I stepped inside. Two wine bottles on the coffee table, two empty wineglasses. No one in the front room. Peering into the short hall, I could see that Ann-Marie's bedroom door was closed.

I took a deep breath and let it out. Thank goodness.

She had gone to bed. I didn't have to decide whether or not to tell her about Lou.

I glanced at my watch. Nearly three-thirty. No wonder I felt so tired. I'm a working girl. I'm not used to these hours.

I crossed the hall and entered my room, clicking on the ceiling light. Yawning, I dropped my bag onto the dresser top. I undid my earrings, pulled them off, and set them down next to my bag.

Feeling a breeze on my back, I turned away from the dresser and saw that the window was wide open. The half-drawn shade flew into the room, then flapped back against the window frame. I squinted at the window, trying to remember if I had opened it.

No. I remembered deliberately leaving it shut because the forecast had said rain. It was a stuffy, humid night. Had Ann-Marie opened it for me to cool off my room?

I usually kept the window locked because it opened onto a fire escape. I'd been trying to get the super to put bars in the window. I didn't feel safe without them. Anyone could climb down the fire escape from the roof or up from the alley behind the building, and step right into my room.

I shuddered. I had a frightening hunch. Someone had climbed into my room. Someone was hiding in the closet. Such a strong hunch . . .

I yanked open the closet door, preparing to scream.

No one.

Way to go, Lindy. Now you're frightening *yourself*. Get to bed. It's been a long night.

I crossed to the window and felt rain floating in on the warm night air. I closed it and locked it, straightened the shade, and turned back to the dresser. I glimpsed myself in the mirror. The pink lipstick had faded away, leaving my lips dry and chapped. I had dark blue lines under my eyes, and my skin was pale. I looked like the *ghost* of Lindy Sampson.

And I felt so grimy and sticky. I'll shower in the morning, I decided.

I started to pull off my pink T-shirt when I noticed the middle dresser drawer half open. Strange. I have a thing about always pushing my dresser drawers shut. No reason. It's just one of the things I do, like making my bed every morning.

I gazed down at the half-open drawer. My underwear drawer. I pulled it open all the way—and uttered a sharp gasp.

Empty.

Where were my panties and bras? I blinked a few times, as if that would fill the drawer up again. But no. It took me a while to see the envelope, a legal-sized white envelope standing against the back of the drawer.

"What the hell is this?"

I lifted it out, tore it open, and pulled out a letter. I scanned it quickly, then read it twice before the words began to make sense. Then the letter shook in my hand as I read it—slowly—for a third time:

I thought a beautiful girl like you would have nicer underwear. Did you get my phone message? I am going to kill you, Lindy. It's not a joke. I will kill you.

There's only one way to stay alive. Keep going out with me. Keep saying yes.

Don't think you can escape me. I've been in your room. I may be watching you right now.

Keep seeing me. Don't ever say no.

Your life depends on it.

Love, ALWAYS

PART THREE

19

I burst into Ann-Marie's room screaming, "You've got to help me. Someone's been in my room!"

I clicked on the ceiling light. She was sprawled on the bed on her stomach, her arms straight out at her sides, dressed in her top and skirt. She hadn't even managed to take off her shoes.

"Ann-Marie? Ann-Marie? Can you hear me? Are you alive?"

She stirred, raised her head, struggled to open her eyes. "No thanks. I've had enough," she whispered.

"Ann-Marie, I need help. I've—I've been robbed! Wake up! Please—!"

She raised her head and squinted up at me with one bloodshot eye. "Huh?"

"Someone was in our apartment! I've been robbed!"

Ann-Marie sat up and blinked at me, hair falling in damp tangles over her face. "You're serious?"

"Yes. Come with me." I tried to tug her to her feet.

"Ohmigod. Lindy, they were in your room? What did they take? Did they get your mother's rings?" She shook herself awake. "Give me a sec. I'll be right there. Oh, wow. Are you okay? You're shaking."

"I'm scared," I said. "I mean, he climbed in the window. He was in my room. And the note . . . He left a note . . ." The words caught in my throat. "Annie, he took all my underwear!"

"Huh? Underwear? I have to pee. I'll be right there." She stumbled to her feet.

I ran back into my room and dropped onto the edge of the bed. I took several deep breaths, trying to slow my racing heartbeats.

I stared at the window. I tried to picture someone climbing in. Someone with a letter for me. Someone carrying a bag or a backpack to carry away my things.

Someone I knew.

Yes. One of the guys I'd been out with.

A chill ran down my back. One of them had sneaked into my apartment. Threatened to kill me.

I don't want to sleep in this room, I decided. I feel so invaded, I don't want to be in this room anymore. I could run away. I could disappear. That would show the sick creep, wouldn't it? All his planning and threatening for nothing.

My eyelids felt heavy. The room began to sway in front of me. I steadied myself on the bed with both hands. Then I picked up the note and read it one more time.

It was so . . . cold. The whole tone of it. The guy who wrote it *hated* me. It was obvious. But then if he hated me so much, why did he want to keep on going out with me?

Was it just a sick power trip?

I pulled myself to my feet and carried the note to the dresser. I dropped it back into the open drawer where I'd found it. Had I touched the drawer handles? Had I ruined any fingerprints the guy might have left? Maybe. I'd touched the window, too.

Police don't really use fingerprints much, do they? Isn't that only on TV?

I knew I wasn't thinking clearly. My panic had given way to total exhaustion. I pulled off my clothes, tossing them onto the floor, and grabbed a nightshirt from my top drawer.

At least the guy left me my nightshirts.

Brad? Colin? Jack?

I pictured their faces as I stared at the empty dresser drawer. A hand grabbed my shoulder. I cried out.

"Sorry," Ann-Marie said. "Didn't mean to scare you." She had run cold water on her face, and her mascara had run onto her cheeks. She had tied back her hair. Taken off her shoes and stockings.

"Look," I said, pointing into the drawer. "All my underwear. Gone."

"Jesus." She picked up the envelope. "This is the note?"

I nodded. "It's so . . . horrible."

Ann-Marie held the note close to her face and squinted at it, frowning, as she read it. She read it twice, then dropped it onto the dresser top. Then she turned and wrapped me in a hug. "Lindy, I'm so sorry. So sorry I got you into this."

"Oh, it's not your fault," I said. "I just don't understand—"

"Lou and I got back here a little after one," she said, backing away from me and pacing the small room. She glimpsed herself in my dresser mirror. "Ugh." She spun away, rubbing at the mascara stains on her cheeks.

"And did you hear anything at all?" I asked.

She shook her head. "No. Nothing. But we had music on pretty loud. And we were . . . kinda out of it. You know."

I swallowed. "I just can't believe someone I know would do this. He says he'll kill me. He'll kill me if I don't say yes to him."

Ann-Marie pulled me away from the dresser. "Don't touch anything, Lin. The police will want to check for fingerprints, right?" She glanced at the window. "Did you leave it open when you went out tonight?"

"No," I said, sighing. "He must have opened it from outside and climbed in."

Ann-Marie hugged me again. "Sit down. You look very pale."

I shook my head. "Jack? Brad? Oh shit, Annie. What if it's Colin? What if I slept with a killer?"

Ann-Marie pulled me to the edge of the bed and forced me to sit down. Then she handed me the phone. "Go ahead. Call the police. Tell them someone broke in."

I hesitated, staring at the phone.

What if it's Colin?

Are you the guy, Colin?

"Should I call them for you?" Ann-Marie asked. "Want me to do it?"

"No," I said in a whisper. "No no no."

Because I'd figured it all out.

No need to call the police. It suddenly became clear.

"What's wrong, Lin?" Ann-Marie asked, leaning over me. "Why don't you want to call them?"

I had to force out the words. "Because I know who it was."

She blinked at me and lowered the phone.

"I figured it out," I whispered. "I know I'm right."

"Who?" Ann-Marie asked softly. "Tell me."

"I'm really sorry, Annie," I said. "I'm so so sorry. Really. But . . . it was Lou."

20

Ann-Marie froze. She stared at me open-mouthed. Then she tossed the phone onto the bed and loomed over me. "No way! Are you crazy?"

I climbed off the bed and took a few steps back. "I'm sorry. Sorry. Sorry."

"You've lost it," she said, balling her hands into tight fists. "Are you stoned, too? How could it be Lou? Why would you even suspect Lou? I was with him all night. Remember? I was with him the whole time."

My heart raced. My legs were trembling. I didn't want to have this scene. But I knew I was right.

"Do you remember saying goodnight to him?" I asked.

She tilted her head and stared at me as if she didn't understand the question. "Say goodnight? Yes, of course. I mean . . . I mean . . . no."

"You don't remember," I said, "because you went to bed. You were already flat out on your bed when I came in."

"So? What does that mean? Lou and I got a little high. Big fucking deal. And I passed out for a little while. But that doesn't prove anything, Lin. Just because Lou was alone in the apartment? How the hell does that make him a thief and a killer?"

"You . . . don't understand," I stammered. I didn't want to go ahead with this, but I had no choice. "This is hard for me, Ann-Marie. I . . . I don't want to do this, but—"

"Then don't," she snapped angrily. "You know I'm here to help you, Lin. I'll do anything I can for you. But if you're going to try to ruin things between Lou and me—"

"Lou came on to me, Ann-Marie." The words burst from my mouth. "He practically attacked me. He grabbed my breasts and . . . and said horrible things."

Her eyes darted rapidly from side to side. "Where? When?"

"He was leaving when I got home. He came out of the apartment and cornered me in the hall. He said horrible things. I thought he was going to—"

"He was just high," Ann-Marie cried. "He didn't mean anything. He was loaded."

"Listen to me, Ann-Marie. Lou was alone in the apartment. He was the only one who—"

"Why are you trying to hurt me?" she cried, her voice breaking. "Lindy, why are you doing this? The first guy I've been so crazy about? And you want to accuse him with no evidence at all?"

"Annie, please—"

.

Her features tightened into a cold mask. "What did you do?" she demanded, lowering her voice to a growl. "Did you come on to him? That's it, isn't it. You stuck your tits in his face and came on to him. Why, Lin? I thought I was your best friend. All those guys, and you have to have Lou, too?"

I could see I was getting nowhere. I wished I hadn't brought Lou up at all. I suddenly felt so weary. I knew I was right about Lou. But I had to stop this argument. I had to calm Ann-Marie.

"Sorry," I whispered. I reached out to her, but she turned away, crossing her arms in front of her. "I guess I took it wrong," I said. "He was trashed, and I was so tired. I'm sorry. You're right. There's no reason to sus-pect Lou. I'm just so scared, Annie. Please be under-standing. Please—I really need a friend now. Don't be angry. I had it all wrong."

Her expression softened. "Lou is a sweetheart, Lin. I know he's gruff sometimes. Maybe he's cruder and less sophisticated than your friends. But he's a sweet guy, and I'm crazy about him."

"Sorry," I whispered again. "I need to sleep. I know I'll think a lot clearer in the morning. Please forgive me, Ann-Marie. Please. I'm so sorry."

She nodded, but without warmth.

That was totally stupid of me, I thought. Now Ann-Marie will be up all night, angry at me, wondering about Lou.

The police can wait till tomorrow morning, I decided.

I climbed into bed and pulled the sheet and blanket up
to my chin.

That was so stupid. So totally stupid.

But I knew I was right.

Why did you do it, Lou?

21

I awoke a little after nine, warm yellow sunlight pouring over my bed. I sat up groggily, knowing I had something to feel uneasy about, not quite remembering.

The open dresser drawer brought it all back.

I showered, put on a pair of baggy, khaki Banana Republic shorts and a turquoise pullover, tugged on a matching turquoise hair scrunchie and fixed my hair into a ponytail.

I checked Ann-Marie. She hadn't moved—still face-down on the bed, breathing noisily. Luisa hadn't come home. Probably hooked up with some guy she met at the bar.

I gulped down a glass of orange juice, drank it too fast. I shut my eyes against the pain in my forehead. When it subsided, I stared at the blank, white refrigerator across the room and tried to make a list in my mind, a list of my thoughts:

* It definitely could have been Lou. He opened the bedroom window to make it look as if someone

came from outside. But was he carrying a bag or anything?

* I never should have told Ann-Marie my suspicion. I should have checked it out first. *Got to confront Lou.* That's the best way to handle it. *But will he only deny it?*

* What if I'm wrong? Lou frightened me last night, and said such ugly things, and seems the likely thief. But I've never said yes to him before. Why would he write for me to *keep on* saying yes?

* I wasn't thinking clearly last night. Lou might not be the one.

* And it couldn't be Shelly. I was with him the whole time last night. He was barely out of my sight for a minute.

* So who does that leave?

Last night I'd felt so certain it was Lou, it had been comforting in a way. I had it solved. No problem. But this morning, in the light of day, as they say, I realized I didn't know anything.

Ann-Marie was right. I had no choice but to call the police. I found my phone directory and punched in the number of the Eighty-second Street station.

Tommy came on the line after only a few minutes' delay. He seemed very surprised to hear from me again. "I didn't think the phone message you played for me last week was serious, Lindy. Guess I was wrong."

Yeah, guess so, Tommy.

Half an hour later, I was sitting in a folding chair in

front of his gun-metal-gray desk, watching him scratch his thinning hair as he read the intruder's letter. He was wearing a faded yellow, short-sleeved sports shirt, open at the neck, and khaki Dockers. "I'm not really on today," he explained when he ushered me inside the cubicle-sized office. "But what the hell? Where else do I have to go?"

I laughed and then realized he didn't mean it to be funny. The hangdog expression and stooped posture were new. When Ben was his partner, Tommy seemed a lot sharper, more alive. Maybe he had just been younger.

He read the letter a couple of times, wrinkling and unwrinkling his forehead. When he finished, he examined the paper, as if it would reveal some important clue.

"Too bad he didn't handwrite it," he said. He lifted the cardboard coffee cup off his desk, saw that it was empty, and tossed it into the trash basket next to me. "Sometimes they handwrite 'em, and it's a real help."

"So, are we taking this one seriously?" I asked. I shifted my weight on the folding chair. I felt awkward sitting there in front of the cluttered desk. I didn't know what to do with my hands.

Tommy nodded. "Well, we have a crime here. We have to take it seriously. It's breaking and entering. And there's a theft. And a death threat. Yeah, that's serious. I'll get a couple crime scene boys over there this morning. They'll do a thorough job."

He frowned and picked up the letter again. "So the window was wide open onto the fire escape. Check?"

"Check."

"And the dresser drawer was empty and left open. Check?"

"Check."

"And what about footprints? You got carpet in that room, right? I seem to remember . . ."

"Yes. It's sort of light red, kind of pink. Almost wall-to-wall, not quite. Pretty thin and faded. It was left there by the last tenant, and I was too lazy to take it out."

"And the footprints?"

"I didn't see any, Tommy."

"But it rained last night, right? Actually, it was pouring. So the guy's shoes had to be wet."

I shrugged. "I'm pretty sure I would have noticed. I didn't see any prints. No mud. Nothing."

"My guys'll check it out. Anything else in the room get moved?"

"I don't think so."

He turned to the laptop on his desk and typed for a while. "Just taking notes. You want some coffee, Lindy? A Danish, maybe?"

"Don't all cops eat doughnuts?"

"Ha ha."

Ben ate doughnuts, I remembered. He was so excited when the Krispy Kreme opened on Seventy-second Street. That night, I thought the box he carried into the apartment contained a pizza. Instead, it was six cream-filled and six custard-filled.

"And do you want to hear the best part?" Ben asked,

leaning over the box, practically *inhaling* the doughnuts. "They deliver! I put the phone number on my cell."

It didn't take much to make Ben happy . . .

"So? Coffee?"

"No thanks, Tommy. My stomach is kind of tied up in knots."

"Well, this isn't nice," he said, tapping the letter. "But we'll get the guy. I'm gonna put my best team on it. You already gave me a list of guys." He pulled a pad out of a desk drawer and began flipping through it. "I have 'em in here. I'll have to enter them in the computer now."

He stopped halfway through the little notebook. "Hey, what about the window? Was it locked when you left the apartment last night?"

"I . . . don't remember. I know it was closed. I usually lock it."

"Usually?"

I nodded. "But I might have forgotten. It was hot during the day, right? And the only air conditioner is in the livingroom. So I might have had my window open during the day."

"But not when you left?"

"No, it was definitely closed."

"And the window wasn't broken when you found it open last night?"

I bit my bottom lip. "No. The window was fine."

"No damage of any kind?"

"No."

"So maybe the window was opened from the inside?"

"Maybe. Maybe Ann-Marie opened it to let in some air."

"Lindy, did you ask her?"

"No."

Tommy typed something on the laptop. He had long fingers and they didn't seem to fit on the keys. He kept making mistakes and backing up. "Well, we'll have to ask her if she opened the window."

I took a breath. "There was one other person in the apartment last night. Ann-Marie's boyfriend. He . . . well . . . I think you need to check him out, too, Tommy."

"Name?"

"Lou D'Amici."

Tommy typed the name into his laptop.

"He's Ann-Marie's new boyfriend. Lou was there very late. I bumped into him leaving as I was coming home."

A thin smile spread over Tommy's face. "And was he carrying a bag of underwear when he left?"

"You are *so* not funny," I said. "You're not supposed to make me laugh. Someone wants to kill me."

His smile faded. "So who do you think it is? Tell me. Do you think it's this guy, Lou D'Amici?"

I shrugged again. "Maybe. I don't know."

He leaned closer. I could smell his Old Spice shaving lotion. Ben wore it, too. "Come on. Think about it. You probably have a hunch. And nine times out of ten, it's right."

"I really don't know. Honest. Last night . . . I thought it was definitely Lou. But it doesn't make sense. I . . . I'm just totally mixed up, Tommy."

He nodded. "Any one of the Internet guys pestering you more than the others? You know. Emailing a lot. Calling. Any guy pursuing you more than the others?"

"Well . . . Jack Smith. He emails me every day. And he calls at least twice a day."

Tommy squinted at his notes. "Jack Smith. Twenty-five years old. Has a condo in Hoboken. Works for Smith-Warner-Conyers Public Relations. His daddy's firm. Never been married. Graduated from Wesleyan with a 2.8. No police record."

I patted his hand. "You've been doing some home-work. Thanks."

He waved a fly off his stack of files. "I haven't had time to work up profiles on all of them. This guy Shelly . . ."

"Shelly Olsen? You can cross him off the list, Tommy. He's the only one who *couldn't* have done it," I said.

"And why is that?"

"Because I was out with him last night. He was barely out of my sight from seven-thirty until I got home. No way he could have been in my room."

I told Tommy how Shelly and I had dinner at the hot dog stand, then went downtown to Whale for hours. The only time Shelly was away from my side was to go buy us drinks at the bar or go to the men's room. He was never gone long enough to go uptown and back.

"Okay, Shelly has a good alibi," Tommy agreed. He typed some more on the laptop. The phone rang. He answered it, turning away from me to talk. He talked to another cop for a few minutes while I waited with my hands clasped in my lap, thinking about the two remaining guys.

Was there a clue I was missing? Was there something I should have noticed? Something in my room last night? Something one of the guys said?

Tommy finally hung up the phone. He bent to open his bottom desk drawer, pulled out his gun and holster, then climbed to his feet. "Gotta go on patrol. A guy called in sick."

I stood up, too. I'd had my legs tightly crossed, and my right foot had fallen asleep. I shook it, trying to get the feeling back. "So what do you think, Tommy?"

He strapped on the leather holster, then slid a wrinkled brown sports jacket over his shoulder. "I'm going to work up complete profiles on these three Internet guys. And Lou D'Amici, too. And I'll send my crime scene guys to your apartment this morning to check out your room and talk to your roommate."

He started to the front of the station, taking long strides. I chased after him, gimpy on my tingling foot. "Hey, wait, Tommy. What should I do if these guys call or email me and ask me out? What should I do?"

He turned at the front desk. "Just say no, Lindy. That's my advice. Just say no to all of them."

I stared at him. "You mean—?"

He narrowed his eyes at me. "Lose them," he said. "Tell 'em all to take a hike. Tell them you got married or something." He disappeared out the door.

But, wait, I wanted to say, *Tommy, won't that put me in a lot of danger?*

22

I walked home and found Ann-Marie awake, or rather, conscious, hunched at our kitchen table in torn jeans and a baggy, gray sweatshirt, a mug of coffee pressed to her mouth. She blinked at me. She had a row of colored pills lined up in front of her. She takes vitamins and mineral tablets and weird supplements she buys at the health food store. She believes in that stuff.

"Lindy? When did you go out? Where were you?"

"With Tommy Foster at the precinct house. You were right, Ann-Marie. I need the police. I'm really sorry about last night, about what I said. I mean, Lou—"

"Did he really come on to you, Lin?"

Yes, he did. Yes, he groped me and said horrible things about you. But I could see tears glistening in Ann-Marie's eyes. What was the point in hurting her?

"I don't know," I said. "Not really, I guess. I mean, he was so trashed, Ann-Marie, he didn't know what he was saying. Let's forget about it, okay? I'm really sorry. I was so messed up last night. Will you accept my apology?"

She nodded.

Before we could say any more, the doorbell rang. Two blue-uniformed officers from the Eighty-second Street station. We spent the rest of the morning with them. One of them questioned Ann-Marie and me, writing down everything we said. He gave me a Crime Report sheet to fill out.

The other one examined my room. He picked up hair samples from the carpet. He dusted the dresser and the window handles with a white powder. For fingerprints, I guess. His partner climbed out on the fire escape to search for clues on the metal stairs.

It was a lot like *CSI* on TV, only it was my life—and the story wasn't over in an hour.

Luisa returned home a little before noon, and they questioned her, too. She kept gazing over the officers' shoulders at me, questioning me with her eyes. I could tell what she was thinking: *Is this for real?*

When the cops left, they took my answering machine with them. It still had the original message on it, and they wanted to listen to it carefully at the station.

I thanked them and closed the door and turned to my roommates. "I have to get out of here," I said. "I can't stay in this apartment one more minute."

"Okay, I'm ready," Luisa said. "Where should we go?"

"Maybe a lingerie store," I said. "How long can I wear this same pair of panties?"

Ha ha. Keep laughing, right?

We went jogging instead, along the Hudson River in Riverside Park. The sun was high in the sky, making the water sparkle like gold, and the high clouds above us glowed silvery and pink, a glorious afternoon. But I kept turning back, looking behind me, checking to see if I was being followed.

I was becoming totally paranoid. But I had good reason, right? I mean, someone had threatened to kill me last night.

I explained the whole thing to Luisa as we jogged. She still hadn't gotten over the shock of finding two cops searching the apartment when she got home.

"Just say no to them all?" Luisa said, brushing a bug from her black hair. She had a strange way of running. Most people lean forward when they jog, but she kept her upper body very upright, as if she were riding a unicycle. "That's your cop's advice? He really thinks the guy will forget you and just go on to some other poor victim?"

"He thinks it's safer," I said, dodging a Golden Lab on a very long leash. The dog was sniffing the air, pushing against the tall, wire fence to get to the water down below.

Luisa frowned at me. "I'm not so sure."

"Luisa's right," Ann-Marie said. "Wouldn't it be safer to keep saying yes until the cops catch the guy? I mean, if the note is serious. If the creep means it, shouldn't you keep saying yes?"

I sighed. "I don't know. I'm totally confused. I'm in

danger either way, right?" I felt out of breath, my legs heavy and slow. I'd been skipping my gym days. The waist on my bike shorts felt a little tight.

"I'll bet it's the boring one," Ann-Marie said, her eyes on two ducks bobbing in the water. "Jack Smith. It's always the boring ones who murder people. And then the neighbors say, 'He was quiet and kept to himself, seemed like such a nice guy.'"

We passed the Seventy-ninth Street Boat Basin, white houseboats tethered to the long dock, bobbing gently on the soft river current. A tanned man in a black swimsuit waved to us from a boat halfway down the dock. "Hey, girls—I've got cold beer! Come on down! I've got cold beer!"

We laughed. Ann-Marie waved at him, and we kept jogging. Above us on the right, music floated out from a café overlooking the water. I took a deep breath. I love the smell of cheeseburgers being barbecued, that heavy, greasy smell. Since it's outdoors, the café is one of the few restaurants in New York where people can bring their dogs, and I could hear them barking away, begging for cheeseburger scraps and french fries.

"It's not the boring one. It has to be the one you like," Luisa said, adjusting her sweatband. "What's his name? Colin?"

"Yeah. Colin." I wanted to see him again. I wanted to feel his arms around me again. It couldn't be Colin. How could I say no to him? When he calls again, how could I say no?

Luisa shook her head. "Big mistake. Your cop friend is totally whacked. He's setting you up to be murdered."

"Oh, wow. Thanks a heap." I stopped running. I glared at Luisa angrily. "Thanks for trying to cheer me up."

She turned, pulling her headband off, shaking out her hair. "Cheer you up? Lindy, hel-lo. I'm trying to save your life. Don't listen to that cop. Say yes to these guys. Yeah, maybe it'll be a little dangerous. But you'll be able to tell who the creep is. You'll know right away. And then the cops can put the guy away."

"Hey, I'm with you," Ann-Marie said to Luisa, bending to catch her breath, hands on the knees of her tights. "She has to say yes. She has to believe the note was for real. She's in much more danger if she says no."

"We've got to stop arguing about this," I said. I felt my throat tighten. "What's the point? I mean, there's one thing we agree on, right? I'm in danger."

Ann-Marie glanced around. Her whole body shuddered. "The guy was in our apartment. Maybe we *all* are in danger."

Stepping into the apartment filled me with dread. But I knew I'd have to get over it. We headed right to the fridge. Luisa and I grabbed bottles of Rolling Rock. Ann-Marie poured herself a glass of apple juice. A new health kick?

We sat down at the kitchen counter. The phone rang in my room.

My hand shot out and knocked over my beer bottle. The cold beer puddled on the Formica countertop, then poured into my lap. I jumped to my feet.

"Just lick it up," Luisa said.

My phone rang again. I turned toward my room. No answering machine to pick up.

"Don't get it," Ann-Marie said. She grabbed a handful of napkins and began dabbing at the spilled beer.

"I have to get it," I said, my heart thudding. "My dad usually calls on Sunday."

"But if it's the creep—?"

"I'll invite him over for brunch."

Ann-Marie's mouth dropped open.

Ha ha. Here's Lindy, making jokes when she's actually shaking with fright.

Well, I don't want to shake and tremble and spill my drink every time the phone rings. I'm not going to let some stupid creep make me afraid to answer the phone.

I grabbed it off my dresser and clicked it on, feeling more anger than fear. "Hello!" I practically screamed the word.

Silence at the other end. Then a throat being cleared. "Hello? Hello?"

Soft, steady breathing.

Oh no. Damn. Damn. Damn. Not again.

"Who is this? Who the hell is this?"

Hoarse breathing, rapid now.

"Stop calling me! Just stop!" I shouted. "The . . . the police are tracing this call. They'll be there in a few minutes. No lie. They're tracing the call."

A soft whisper: "Oh, baby . . ."

I clicked it off. My ear hurt from pressing the phone against it so hard. I stared out the window, trying to calm my throbbing heartbeats.

Was it really someone I knew?

Please . . . please let it be a stranger.

Fighting down a wave of nausea, I pressed *69 to trace the call. After a few rings, a machinelike woman's voice droned in my ear: "I'm sorry, but the number you are trying to reach cannot be reached in this way."

I let out an angry cry and tossed the phone onto my bed.

"Who was it?" Ann-Marie hurried into my room.

I shook my head. "The breather again. It was so totally gross. Why is this happening to me?"

Before Ann-Marie could answer, the phone rang again.

I could feel all my muscles tighten. "That fucking creep!" I seethed. I grabbed the phone and clicked it on. "Listen, you son of a bitch—!

". . . Oh. Hi, Dad. Sorry about that."

23

Emails . . . emails . . .

Brad emailed. Said he had really good seats for the Allman Brothers at the Beacon Friday night.

The Allman Brothers come every year to play for two weeks at the Beacon, a huge, converted movie theater in my neighborhood, and it's a wild scene. The audience is bizarre and the band rocks them into a frenzy that usually spills out onto the streets afterward.

An interesting invitation. But of course I emailed back and said the *N*-word. The big NO. I gave a lame excuse about having to visit a cousin in Forest Hills.

I didn't say anything like, "I don't think we should see each other again," or, "I'm getting serious about someone, so I have to say goodbye."

Frankly, I was scared to do that. I followed Tommy Foster's instruction and said no to Friday night. But I was afraid that the one who threatened me would take a final NO as a challenge—a challenge to come get me.

Keep seeing me. Don't ever say no.
Your life depends on it.

I hadn't forgotten the words of the ugly note in my dresser. In fact, I had memorized them. Sometimes I couldn't stop them from repeating and repeating in my mind.

There's only one way to stay alive. Keep going out with me. Keep saying yes.

Only one way to stay alive . . . but I said no to Brad.

And when Jack emailed to say someone had given him tickets to an advanced screening of the new Indiana Jones movie, I said no to that, too.

No, Jack. Can't make it.

Now what? Are you going to kill me?

Isn't this brave of me?

But my hands shook and I missed the keys as I typed my replies.

No, guys. I know I'm supposed to keep saying yes. But Tommy Foster must know what he's doing.

Right?

Monday night, I'm online and Colin IM's me.

COLINOC: Lindy, r you there? How r u?
LINDYSAM: I'm here. Where are you?
COLINOC: Been thinking about you. A lot.
COLINOC: Miss you.
LINDYSAM: Are u in NYC? Where are you?
COLINOC: Would you believe Rochester?

My fingers were wet on the keys. My heart was pounding. I thought about Colin . . . about last weekend. So nice.

Whoa. If Colin was in Rochester Saturday night, that means he couldn't be the one who sneaked into my room. An alibi! And I wouldn't have to say no to Colin.

Yes. An alibi.

LINDYSAM: When did u leave for Rochester?
COLINOC: Been in meetings all day. But kept thinking about you.
COLINOC: You could destroy my career!
LINDYSAM: When did you leave?

Please say Saturday!

COLINOC: Left this morning. Went right to meetings. On to Toronto on Wednesday.

Shit. There goes the alibi.

COLINOC: U need a Webcam so I could see you.
LINDYSAM: Sweet. Gotta run.
COLINOC: Have a wedding next weekend. (Boring.) See you next week? ASAP? How about Saturday night?
LINDYSAM: Email me when you get home. We'll discuss.

I couldn't say no to Colin. I realized I had real feelings for him. By next week, the police might have the creep in custody. And I could be snuggling in Colin's arms in his cozy apartment and telling him all about my frightening week.

I wish.

I hadn't forgotten about Lou. I decided I wanted to confront Lou myself. I had the crazy idea that if I just accused him point-blank of stealing my clothes and leaving the note and calling me up and breathing into my ear, he'd cave immediately and apologize, and that would be the end of it.

Yes, it was a crazy idea. More of a wish than an idea, I guess. But my mind clung to this plan. I needed something to cling to, some kind of hope that I could get out of it easily—and alive.

So I cornered Lou in our apartment Monday after work. He and Ann-Marie were going out for a quick dinner in the neighborhood. Ann-Marie was in her room changing from her work clothes.

He turned away when I entered the room. He had one hand on the front doorknob. I had the distinct feeling he didn't want to see me.

"Lou, we need to talk," I said softly, glancing back to Ann-Marie's door.

He kept his eyes on the floor. "Lindy, I'm sorry about Saturday night," he said, his cheeks bright red.

Was he confessing?

"Sorry?" I said, moving close to him so we could whisper. No point in upsetting Ann-Marie.

"Out in the hall. I think I said some things . . ."

I stared at him. "Well, yes."

"I don't really remember what I said," he whispered. "Annie and I kinda wrecked ourselves. I mean, I hope you don't think I'm a bad guy or anything."

"Well, I don't know *what* to think," I said.

Wow, was *that* honest!

"Annie told me about the break-in," Lou said, finally raising his eyes to me. "That's really cold. I mean, that's out there. This guy is whacked."

"It's scary," I said, studying his face. He seemed totally sincere. Except one thick eyebrow kept sliding up and down on his wide forehead. Revealing that he was tense? That he was lying?

Why am I reading Lou's eyebrows? God, I'm paranoid.

"The police will find the guy," Lou said, tugging an ear. "He's an amateur. They'll get him. That letter he left you was total bullshit. The guy is just fucking with your mind, Lindy."

How do *you* know?

"Hope so," I murmured. My mind was spinning. I had Lou's confession speech all planned for him, and he wasn't cooperating. "It's someone I know," I said. "That's what's so scary."

Lou took my hand. "That'll make it even easier for the cops," he whispered. He had his eyes on my breasts.

I heard a cough, turned, and saw Ann-Marie watching us from her bedroom door. I quickly pulled my hand from Lou's. "You two seem awfully close all of a sudden," she said, wrapping a bright blue fringed shawl over her shoulders.

"We were just talking about stuff," Lou said. He grinned at me. "I love it when she's jealous."

Ann-Marie had the shawl tangled in the strap of her purse. She tugged hard at it. Lou hurried over to help her. "What were you talking about?" she asked.

"Current events," I answered quickly.

I met Shelly for a drink Tuesday after work at a sports bar on Second Avenue. He wore a loose-fitting, navy Polo shirt over khaki cargo pants. He kissed me on the cheek, his blue eyes flashing, and we settled across from each other in a booth at the back.

"How do you know this place?" I asked, straightening my hair.

"It's one of my bingeing places," he said. "I go on weeklong booze binges every few months. I always drink until I'm hospitalized, and this is one of my hangouts."

I stared at him.

He grinned, shaking his head. "That was a joke, Lindy."

"Oh. Sorry." I felt really stupid for not catching on. But it wasn't that great a joke—especially since I didn't know Shelly that well. And after seeing his intense dancing at the club and his "Singing in the Rain" number that night, I could easily believe that he could go overboard sometimes.

I squeezed his hand. "Next time you go on a booze binge, invite me to come along with you."

He laughed. "I can't picture you totally loaded. I mean, actually falling-down drunk."

"Neither can I," I confessed.

"Ha ha. Here's what you'd look like." He jumped out of the booth and did his idea of me, staggering around crazily. He ended the act by falling over a table and landing facedown on the floor.

Two concerned waitresses set down their trays and came running over to help him. Shelly climbed to his feet, brushing off the knees of his cargo pants. "I'm okay," he told the confused waitresses. "I was just imitating her."

They turned their eyes on me. I could feel my face growing hot. "Don't mind him. He has Tourette's," I said.

The waitresses didn't laugh, but at least they turned back to Shelly. "Did you order yet?" one of them, a short, pixyish blonde, asked.

"Is he allowed to drink?" her partner asked me, pointing at Shelly.

"It will calm him down," I said.

Shelly slid back in the booth. I ordered a glass of chardonnay. "Bring me a Corona with lime every ten minutes," Shelly said. "And when I pass out, bring one every fifteen minutes."

The waitress rolled her eyes and walked away.

"The little one is cute," I said.

He narrowed his eyes. "So you're into girls?"

"I just said she was cute, that's all. Let's change the subject. What's up with the Polo shirt? And where's that navy blazer?"

He made an exaggerated sad face. "It died."

"The other night with me? While you were singing in the rain?"

He nodded. "I gave it a hero's burial. Want to have dinner after this? There's a new barbecue place around the corner—"

"I can't, Shelly." I held up my bag. "I have two manuscripts to read tonight."

"Tell me about your work. I'm fascinated," Shelly said. He put his chin in his hand and stared across the table at me.

"Are you making fun of me?"

"No. No way. I really am fascinated. Tell me about children's publishing. Do you all walk around speaking in simple sentences? 'Hi, my name is Lindy. Watch Lindy read. I can read a book.'"

"Very funny."

It took a while, but Shelly finally settled down. I told him about my little cubicle and what I did all day. About my new book series. About Saralynn, the boss, and Rita Belson, the pain-in-the-ass.

"Your arch enemy," Shelly said. "Let's kill her!"

I stared at him. He had an evil grin on his face, his eyebrows sliding up and down. I knew he meant it as a joke. *Of course* he meant it as a joke. But the murder threat—the real murder threat—was always in the back of my mind.

"How shall we kill her? We need to do it in children's book style." He rubbed his hands together gleefully, like a cartoon villain. "How about we force her to eat ten little ducklings? Aren't there ten little ducklings in every children's book?"

"Shut up," I said. "I don't want to talk about killing people with ducklings."

His smile faded. "Sorry. I didn't know you were sensitive about ducklings."

All evening, I'd been debating whether or not to tell Shelly about the mess I was in. I knew he could see that I was edgy, stressed. I felt tempted. It would be nice to have someone to confide in.

Ann-Marie and Luisa were great friends, and they really would do anything for me. But the two of them never agreed about anything, and their arguments about what I should do were driving me crazy and, let's face it, making me feel even more frightened.

So it had been on the tip of my tongue all evening to say, "Shelly, can we be serious for a moment? Something really terrifying is happening to me."

But when he made the joke about killing Rita, something inside me clicked shut. Shelly didn't do anything wrong—it was a stupid joke that anyone else would have brushed off, or maybe joined in—but it closed a door between us. And in that instant I decided to hold it all inside and not tell him anything.

Instead, I said, "So how's *your* writing coming along?"

He blinked and his face fell into a thoughtful, almost troubled expression. "It's coming along," he said, "slowly."

"And what are you working on now?"

He sighed. "I really can't say. It's a short piece. Slice-of-life stuff. Ha ha. That sounds impressive, doesn't it? Sorta artsy?"

"Shelly, you're weird. You really won't let me see anything you've written?"

He shook his head. "I can't. Because it's about ten little ducklings." He burst out laughing at his own dumb joke.

"If I *Google* you, will I be able to find things you've written?"

He frowned. All the color faded from his eyes. "Not really," he said. "Remember, I told you I haven't been published."

"So do you have a job? How do you make a living?"

"Job?" He sneered at me. "No way. I write full-time. I have a very rich Mom. Very rich and very crazy. A real character, but she likes to write checks."

"She supports your writing? That's really nice."

"Yeah, it's nice. I can even pay for these drinks."

I'm going to *Google* him as soon as I get home, I decided. Maybe I'll find out why he doesn't want to show me his work. His whole personality changed when I asked him about his writing. What could he be writing that he'd be ashamed or embarrassed to show me?

"Do you write porno films?" I blurted out.

Oops. Where did *that* come from?

He laughed, eyes sparkling again. "No, I don't. But do you want to make one? My apartment isn't that far away."

"Ha ha. You'll have to talk to my agent."

"Lindy, do you have a porno name? Everyone should have a porno name, don't you agree?"

I laughed. "What's yours?"

"I don't know . . ." He thought for a moment, grinning at me. "Uh . . . Randy Buttcheeks. No. Wait. That's too gay. How about Peter Allday?"

"Yeah, that's good. That has star quality. And what's mine? Uh . . . wow. I've never played this game, Shelly."

"It's a game?"

"How about Lucy Goosey?"

He shook his head. "Pitiful. You'll be a children's book editor for the rest of your life. But a sexy one."

"Thanks for the compliment."

A waitress set down the check on a little tray. "Want to know mine? It's Britney Spheres." She raised her hands to her enormous breasts. "Get it?"

"Thanks for sharing," Shelly said. He opened his wallet and dropped a gold Amex card on the tray. The waitress swooped it up and hurried off with it. "I'll be right back," Shelly said, and headed to the men's room in back.

I lowered my eyes to the table and saw a small card. It had his name on it in blue type. I picked it up. It must have fallen from his wallet. A business card:

SHELLY OLSEN
Sales Manager
D & W Electronics
"The Complete Store for Professionals"

At the bottom, an address on lower Fifth Avenue and a bunch of phone and fax numbers.

I stared at the card, scanning it again.

What did this mean? He worked in an electronics store?

He wasn't a writer? Is that why he was so mysterious about his writing?

Had he lied about being a writer?

I swallowed. If so, what *else* had Shelly lied about?

I saw him returning, snapping his fingers, smiling at me as he crossed the bar.

I crumpled the card in my hand, and dropped it into my bag.

24

A light rain was falling as we stepped out of the bar, just enough rain to dampen the sidewalk and make all the taxis disappear. Where do they all go when the raindrops start to fall?

I kissed Shelly goodbye. He held on to me for a moment, tenderly, and pressed his face against mine. "See you soon," he whispered. And then, as he started to jog away, "You have anything on this weekend?"

"I don't know," I called. And that was certainly the truth.

I walked for a while, heading west on Eighty-sixth Street. The rain felt kind of refreshing, a warm spring shower, and I needed time to think, to try to sort things out. But I couldn't get past that business card of Shelly's.

I asked him point-blank if he had a job to support himself, and he said no, he had a rich mother.

Why would he lie to me about a thing like that? Was he trying to impress me? *I'm a full-time writer, at home all day creating, not a sales manager for an electronics store.* He practically snapped at me when I asked if I could see his writing. Does he write anything at all?

I had met four guys in the past month. Shelly was the one I thought I could trust. I knew he couldn't have been the one who stole my clothes and left that threatening letter. I thought he was the one I could be safe with.

But that one little card changed everything.

In the bar, I tried to carry on our conversation as if nothing had happened. I jabbered on about work and about Rita Belson and the latest drama involving Saralynn. Shelly told some stories about his mother, wacky stunts she had pulled in stores. Like the time when he was a little boy and she stuffed an entire salami down his pants in a grocery store because she had never tried shoplifting before.

I didn't think the story was too funny. But Shelly told it with great glee, and then he joked about how having a salami in his pants gave him an inferiority complex that lasted for years.

I laughed but I didn't feel like it. And I just kept thinking about that card. That little business card.

I wanted to ask him about it. I was *bursting* to ask him about it. But I knew if I accused him of being a liar, I'd never see him again. And I realized I was drawn to him, maybe not in the same physical way I was drawn to Colin, but I didn't want to send him out of my life so soon.

And maybe it was an old card, a card from a previous life that just happened to be tucked in his wallet.

Dream on, Lindy.

The rain had stopped, and I grabbed a taxi and rode home. Central Park was gray in the evening light, but the apple and cherry blossoms were out on the trees, and the air smelled sweet and springy.

I checked my watch as I rode the elevator to floor eleven—a little after seven-thirty. I hoped Ann-Marie was home. Maybe we could grab some dinner. I wanted to tell her about Shelly and his business card, get her take on it.

"Anyone home?" I called as I opened the front door. No answer.

The lights were all on. Ann-Marie usually clicks them off whenever she goes out. And who moved the couch? I wondered. It was positioned at an angle, one end bumping the low glass coffee table.

Was Ann-Marie moving furniture?

I tossed my bag on the floor. "Hey—Annie? Luisa?"

Silence. I could hear the hum of the refrigerator and car horns down on the street through the open window.

With a sigh, I started to my room.

And stopped when I saw the shoe on the floor by the couch. A black running shoe.

Something strange here. And yes, a foot in the shoe. I mean, I didn't see the foot. I saw white socks, a leg.

A leg on the floor.

Behind the couch, the couch at a weird angle.

"No."

The word slipped from my mouth. I realized I had

stopped breathing. I let the air out in a long whoosh and, heart pounding, ran to the other side of the couch.

And dropped down beside Ann-Marie.

"Can you hear me? Annie? Hey, can you hear me?"

Ann-Marie in maroon sweats, facedown on the carpet, legs spread, one arm beneath her, the other hand gripping the couch fabric as if trying to pull herself up.

And on her arm, the arm I could see, slashes of dark blood, cuts up and down her arm.

"Annie—?"

Eyes shut.

I shook her by the shoulders. "Annie?"

Not breathing.

Not breathing.

Ann-Marie dead on the livingroom floor.

25

Did you really think I was dead?"

Ann-Marie squinted at me, leaning back on the couch as the white-uniformed paramedic bandaged her arm.

"Well . . . yes," I said. "I mean, you were all cut up and—"

"Just my arm." Ann-Marie let out a groan. "No, that's too tight." She turned back to me. "I think maybe I fainted. You know. From fright."

"Well, you gave *me* a fright," I said. "My heart is still doing flip-flops."

The livingroom was crowded now. Two young paramedics arrived less than five minutes after I called 911. One watched as the other treated Ann-Marie's arm.

Two crime scene cops were in my bedroom, checking around the open window where the intruder had apparently entered. Tommy Foster stood in his shirtsleeves, arms crossed in front of him, looking like a sad hound dog, eyes red and circled with black rings. He had brought a young uniformed officer with him, a woman with a headful of bright orange curls, who

stood against the wall, chewing gum rapidly and noisily, staring at her well-shined shoes, waiting for something to happen.

Ann-Marie blinked several times and rubbed the
back of her head. "I think I hit my head when I fell. I
have such a headache."

"We'll give you something for that," the paramedic
said softly. "You won't need this bandage long. The
cuts aren't very deep."

"Can I get you anything?" I asked Ann-Marie.

"Water?"

I hurried to the kitchen. Behind me, I heard Tommy
ask, "Feel like talking? I need to hear what happened."

Ann-Marie sighed. "Yeah. I guess. It all happened so
fast. I don't know how helpful . . ."

"Can you start at the beginning? When did you get
home?"

I handed a water bottle to Ann-Marie and sat down
on the couch next to her. Tommy lowered himself into
the armchair across from us. He motioned to the female
officer, who pulled out a notepad and prepared to write.

"I guess I got home from work around six-thirty or
so," Ann-Marie started. She tilted the bottle to her
mouth and took a long drink. "Maybe a little later."

Tommy leaned forward as if trying to hear better,
his hands on his knees. "And was the intruder waiting
for you?"

Ann-Marie shut her eyes. "I think so. I was in the
kitchen. I had a long day. One of our actors freaked out
on the set, and I had to deal with it. I . . . I wanted a

beer. I pulled open the refrigerator and . . . and then he grabbed me. He—He—" Her voice cracked. She took another long drink.

"He burst into the kitchen, like from out of nowhere. He grabbed my arm—really hard—and pulled me into the livingroom. I kept screaming, 'Who are you? What do you want?' But he didn't say a word. Just dragged me in here. I . . . tried to fight. I tried to get away. But he shoved me into the couch, so hard it slid over the carpet. Then he slapped me."

Tommy rubbed his chin, studying Ann-Marie, not blinking. "What did he look like? Can you give us a physical description? Did you recognize him?"

She shook her head, then winced. "Ow. My head really hurts."

The paramedics had packed up. One of them handed her a container of pills. "Painkillers. Just take one when it hurts. No more than two a day." He handed her a pen, and she signed the form he held out. Then the two of them hurried out of the apartment.

Ann-Marie turned back to Tommy. "I couldn't see him. I mean, he had a thing over his face. You know. A mesh stocking. Very thick. I couldn't see his features."

Tommy frowned. "Was he tall? Short?"

"Tall. And average weight, not fat or anything and not skinny. He was strong."

"What was he wearing?" Tommy asked.

"All black. He had like a black sweater and a black T-shirt under it and black denims. And the stocking on his face. I tried to rip it off him, but he was too strong. He didn't look it, but he was really strong."

She took a long drink of water. Water spilled down her chin. She wiped it away with her other hand. "Lindy, could you hand me one of these pills?"

"No problem." My hands shook as I struggled to open the pill bottle. Ann-Marie's story was terrifying. Someone waiting in our apartment for her to get home.

Or *was* he waiting for her?

Was he waiting for *me*?

"So what did he do?" Tommy asked. "Did he ever say anything?"

Ann-Marie nodded. "Oh, yes. After he slapped me, he held me down, against the back of the couch. He pulled out this tool . . . a knife thing. You know. A box cutter or whatever. And he sliced me with it. Sliced my arm."

Tommy narrowed his eyes at her. "He didn't say anything? Just cut you with a box cutter?"

"Yes. I screamed. It hurt a lot. I begged him to let me go. And he . . . cut me again. And again. And then he . . . well . . . he pulled me to my feet and pressed his face against mine. I was so frightened. My legs were shaking. I didn't think I could stand. My arm was bleeding. And he held the box cutter up to my face."

"Ohmigod." I dropped the pill I was about to hand Ann-Marie. I felt sick. I dropped to my knees on the rug and searched for it.

"He slammed his face against mine," she continued. "The stocking rubbed my skin. I could feel him through the stocking. His face was really hot. I . . . I thought he was going to rape me. But he whispered . . . whispered in my ear. 'Tell her not to say no. Tell her this is what happens if she says no.' "

Oh, Jesus. So it *was* about me. Poor Ann-Marie. This happened to her because I said no to two of the guys.

"Is that all he said?" Tommy asked.

Ann-Marie nodded. "That was all. Just, 'Tell her this is what happens.' Then he cut my arm again and shoved me hard. And . . . I guess I fainted. Fell to the floor." She took a long drink of water.

"Son of a bitch," the female officer muttered behind us.

Tommy continued to stare at Ann-Marie. "Can you remember anything else? About the way he looked or something he did or something else he said? Think hard. Anything else at all?"

Ann-Marie stared back at Tommy, her mouth open, thinking. "Well . . . no. Not really. I don't think . . . Well . . . I do remember one thing. When he pushed his face against mine, I could feel his beard. He had a really thick, bristly beard. I could feel it right through the stocking."

PART FOUR

26

"Yes, it's based on *King Lear,* that's obvious," Colin said. "But Kurosawa has expanded it, at least visually. And his world view is so much darker than Shakespeare's."

"The battle scenes were overwhelming," I said. "And the color. Incredible. I saw *Seven Samurai* in college, and I couldn't believe it. But to see him work in color . . . wow."

Colin and I had just seen the Kurosawa film *Ran* at the Film Forum on Houston Street. Yes, it was the following Saturday, and here I was, out with Colin. Saying yes to Colin and not feeling the way I did about him a week ago.

In fact, I had to work hard to hide my fear. But I was following instructions now. Tommy Foster's instructions. He had a whole new strategy for catching the creep who was threatening me.

"Say yes to them," Tommy had said. "There are only a few of them. This won't take long. Say yes to them,

Lindy. The guy will give himself away. You'll know who it is."

"Are you crazy?" I screamed. "Have you totally lost it? You want to send me out there as bait?"

He nodded. "Yes, I do."

"And then what happens when the guy takes out his box cutter and goes for me?" I asked. "Ann-Marie said he's really strong. What happens when he starts slicing me?"

Tommy motioned with both hands for me to calm down. "Lindy, I'll have someone there," he said softly. "You call me when you're going out. I'm giving you my cell number. You call and tell me your plans. And I'll have someone wherever you go. Don't look for them. Don't give it away. They'll be there. They'll be ready to take this guy. This is a no-brainer. Really. We'll have him, I promise."

Was I thrilled with the new plan? I don't think so.

Colin emailed as soon as he got back in town— assuming he had left town to begin with—and I said yes to a movie and dinner Saturday night. Yes, yes, Mr. Scratchy Beard.

And then I was on the phone to Tommy to make sure I wasn't going out alone. And then I thought maybe I could get even more protection. I begged Ann-Marie and Lou to come along, to double with me.

Lou agreed it was a smart idea. But Ann-Marie couldn't do it. Too frightened, she said. She couldn't sit down to dinner with the creep who cut her and terrified her. Besides, her headaches hadn't gone away. The painkillers weren't helping.

"I want to help you," she said, massaging the back of her neck. "I desperately want to help end this thing, Lindy. But please don't ask me to do this. I just can't."

I understood. I guess.

So I went out solo Saturday night, and I wished things could be the same between Colin and me. He seemed so happy to see me and kept talking about how much he thought about me during his business trip . . . thought about the two of us making love in his apartment.

And I stared at the shadow over his face, the black, stubbly beard, and thought, Why did it have to be you?

I tried but I couldn't concentrate on the Kurosawa film. Colin had his arm around my shoulders and kept leaning his head against me. He kissed me a few times, and each kiss sent chills down my body—not the right kind of chills, the chills that tighten all your muscles and make you want to scream.

How sad.

I really liked him, liked him enough to sleep with him on our first date, which isn't like me. And now I felt so mixed up, repelled and drawn to him and unable to have any real feelings at all, tense and numb, and watching . . . watching every move, alert to any sign, to anything that would give him away.

After the movie, we stepped out onto Houston Street, and he hailed a cab. "Where are we going?" I asked, unable to hide my suspicion.

He grinned at me. "It's a surprise."

Surprise? No. I don't want any surprises. I'm not happy about this.

And then we were in a taxi taking us way downtown, through narrow dark streets, to the bottom of the island near Ground Zero.

I couldn't help myself. I gazed through the back window. Is anyone following us? Tommy promised someone would be here. But where are they?

Holding my hand, Colin led me to a tiny Italian restaurant, Giginos, with red and green banners in the window and twinkling red lights. It looked ready for Christmas even though this was the last week in May.

We stepped inside, warm and noisy and bustling, loud voices, lots of laughter, and the overpowering aroma of garlic and tomato sauce. Walking under red and green crepe banners strung from the ceiling, the white-aproned waiter led us to a table the size of a checkerboard near the back.

Colin ordered a bottle of Chianti, saying, "You have to drink really cheap Chianti in a restaurant like this." He made a toast: "To new beginnings," of all things. I only pretended to sip the wine. I wanted to stay alert. I *had* to stay alert. I glanced around the nearby tables. No one sitting alone. No one who looked like a cop.

My heart fluttered in my chest. Am I all alone here?

We settled in to discuss the movie. When the waiter delivered our food, linguini with white clam sauce for me, veal marsala for Colin, we were still discussing it.

"Would you like cheese?" The waiter held a bowl of

parmesan over my food. I shook my head, and he nodded approvingly and disappeared.

"How did you find this restaurant?" I asked, picking
up a clamshell, prying out the clam with a fork, and
tasting it. "Mmmm. Nice and garlicky. It's so far
downtown."

"My old job, my office was two blocks from the
North Trade Tower," he said, slicing his veal. "This
place was just a couple of blocks away, so we used to
have lunch here. It's good, isn't it? I love Northern Italian food, and this is the best place in the city for it, I
think."

"Did you know people who worked at the World
Trade Center?"

He nodded, swallowing. "Yeah. A few."

"Where were you . . . you know . . . that day?"

All New Yorkers remember where they were when
the Trade Towers collapsed, and still talk about it.

He put down his fork. "I was in Chicago, actually. I
was getting dressed to go to some meetings, and I put
on the *Today* Show. I . . . I never made it to the meetings. I just stayed in the hotel room all day watching
TV. It felt so strange being away from the city. I don't
know why, but I felt I should be there, I should be
home."

"I can understand that," I said.

And have you been crazy ever since?

Or did you just decide to go berserk after you met me?

"I had good friends in the North Tower, two women,"
Colin continued. "The first thing I thought about was

them. Did they get out? Were they okay? I tried calling their office, but of course the phones were down. So then I kept calling their cells. They just rang and rang, but no answer."

Colin sighed. He jabbed the veal with his fork. "I think it was the most terrified I've ever been in my life. And, of course, there I was, helpless in a hotel room in Chicago." He swallowed, staring down at his plate.

"So? What happened?" I had to ask since he wasn't finishing the story. "Were they okay?"

"I finally reached one of them that afternoon. They both had climbed down the stairs. They got out. They ran through all the dust and debris. They both just ran. They said they didn't want to stop running. They didn't know how far they had to go to get away, to be safe. One of them said she knew she'd never feel safe again."

"Whoa," I muttered. "She was really messed up? I mean, after . . ."

Colin nodded. "She quit her job. She's seeing a shrink. I don't talk to her as much as before. I always get her machine. She never calls me back."

We started eating again. The food was exceptional. But it just lay heavily in my stomach like a rock. I was too tense to enjoy anything.

I told Colin my 9/11 story, but it wasn't as interesting as his. I was on my way to work on Twenty-third Street. I climbed out of the subway and saw this huge, white plume of smoke in the sky downtown. And I really

didn't think anything of it, figured it was a fire somewhere. So I just walked the rest of the way to work.

"I guess that was like my last innocent moment," I
said. "The world totally changed after that, didn't it?"

He nodded. "Yes. I know I changed a lot. It's weird
but my whole attitude changed after that day. I know it
sounds dorky, but I think I became a different person."

I narrowed my eyes at him. "What was your new attitude?"

A smile spread slowly over his face. "Grab what you
want when you want it. Don't wait for things, because
you don't know how long you really have."

He kept his eyes on me, waiting for my reaction. I
could tell that he had said those words before, in that
very same way.

Grab what you want when you want it?

Why was he studying me like that, staring so intently,
that smile stuck on his face?

"That's an interesting attitude," I said finally. I decided to challenge him. "And what have you been grabbing lately?"

He laughed. "Grabbing a movie and dinner?"

"No, really," I said. "Be serious. You said you decided you should grab what you want and—"

"Well, I went after a better job. And I got it. And . . .
I got out of a bad relationship that had been dragging
on for months."

I swallowed. "I see . . ."

"Before, I know I would have let it drag on. But this

time I didn't. I go after what I want now. And do you
know what else I want?"

"Coffee and dessert?"

He didn't laugh. "No. You." His dark brown eyes
locked on mine. All the humor left his face. Suddenly,
he was totally intense.

A short laugh escaped my throat. "Colin, this is just
part of your new attitude? You want to grab *me* now?"

I didn't mean it to sound so hostile. I wanted it to
sound playful, but it just came out wrong. I could see
the hurt in his eyes.

He narrowed his eyes at me. "Grab you? Lindy . . ."
He slid his hand over mine. "Yes, I'd like to grab you,"
he said softly. "Because I really think you're . . . terrific."

I didn't know how to reply. What was going to happen tonight? I couldn't sleep with him tonight. The
thought made my stomach churn. But what would happen if I said no?

"Come back to my apartment, Lindy. I missed you so
much this week."

I pulled my hand out from under his. What could I
say? How could I say no and make it sound like a yes?

"Coffee and dessert?" The waiter appeared, saving
me for a few moments. He lifted our dinner plates off
the table. "How about a nice espresso?"

I stared at Colin. "Not for me, thanks."

"We're finished. We really enjoyed it. Just bring a
check," Colin told him.

Colin finished the wine in his glass. Then he turned

back to me. "I think you and I could be really good together. I mean, I don't want to sound . . . Look, I really
want you tonight. I want us to really be together,
Lindy."

Wow.

I wanted you, too, Colin—until Ann-Marie described
the guy who slashed her.

I bit my bottom lip. "I . . . can't. Not tonight. I'm
sorry, Colin. Get that hurt look off your face. You
know I like you, too. But . . . I can't tonight."

He smiled, tilting his head to one side. "Is that a no?"

I nodded. "It's a no."

His expression changed. "By the way, did you get
that note I left you?"

27

My mouth dropped open. I felt like screaming.

And then running. Yes. Jump up, turn around, and run out of the restaurant. Don't stop. Don't wait.

You said no to him—so he mentioned the note.

He wants you to know you *can't* say no to him.

Colin watched me calmly, cold-bloodedly. He knew why I suddenly looked so frightened. Was he enjoying my fear?

"Lindy, what's wrong?" All innocence suddenly.

"I . . ." My throat was clogged tight. I couldn't force out the words. "The note . . ."

He gripped the empty wineglass between his hands, smooth, long-fingered hands. Killer's hands?

"Yeah. I sent it to your office. Did you get it?"

My breath caught in my throat. "My office—?"

"It was in a gray envelope? From my company? Blauner and Field?"

"No. I . . . didn't see it."

He wasn't talking about *that* note. He sent me a different note.

Or was he just toying with me? Playing a cat-and-mouse game?

Did he know I'd freak if he mentioned the note? Is that why he asked me about it right after I said no to him? And now he's *pretending* he meant a different note?

Is this some kind of sicko game he likes to play?

"I didn't get your note, Colin. What was it about?" Trying to keep my voice steady and calm.

He shifted in his chair. Was that a sign he was about to tell a lie?

"My company is having a big thing. You know, an office party. For the whole national sales staff. It's like the major party of the year. They're having it at the Met, do you believe it?"

He's telling the truth, I decided. No way he's making this up.

"I wrote this all in the note," he continued. "I wondered if you'd go with me. But if you don't like that kind of thing . . ."

"Well . . ." I hesitated. You might be in prison by then, Colin. "It would be a good excuse to buy a dress," I said, still struggling to make normal conversation.

He scratched his stubbly beard. "Is that a yes?"

"Let me think about it."

I studied his face. It wasn't a twisted person's face. He seemed so sincere. What if I was wrong about him?

No, Lindy. That's not the way to think. You've got to think this way: What if I am *right* about him?

"Is that a maybe?"

I nodded. "Yes. A definite maybe."

He paid the check.

I stood up and glanced around. "I'm going to the ladies' room."

"I'll meet you outside," Colin said. "I'll try to get us a taxi. We're so far downtown it might take awhile."

When I pushed open the front door and stepped out onto the sidewalk, I noticed that the red lights from the restaurant window spilled onto the sidewalk, like puddles of blood. God, now I'm paranoid *and* morbid!

A hot wind blew down the street, fluttering my hair. I shielded my eyes from the dust in the air and waited for them to adjust to the darkness. All the stores were dark and shuttered. No one on the street.

A streetlamp across from the restaurant was out. I could hear the roar of traffic uptown, but no cars moved on this block.

"Colin?" I didn't see him. I took a few steps toward the corner, my shoes thudding the pavement noisily, breaking the silence of the narrow street.

"Colin? Where are you?"

Was he still in the restaurant? Had he gone to the restroom, too?

The wind stopped suddenly, as if someone had turned it off. I could hear tinny music from somewhere far away. A window opened above me at the end of the block.

"Colin? Are you out here?"

I felt a tingle of fear at the back of my neck. We were

so far downtown, nearly at the tip of the island, and no one was around. No cars or taxis. No people on the sidewalk.

Where was my police protection? Tommy had promised someone would be here.

"Hey—Colin!" My voice echoed off the gated storefronts.

I turned back to the restaurant. And saw a figure step into the red puddle of light on the sidewalk.

"Colin—?"

No. The man wore a hood over his head. Squinting hard, I could make out a dark sweatshirt, the hood up, hiding his face, baggy jeans. He moved toward me quickly, arms stiff at his sides.

"Oh. No. Please." I felt my throat tighten.

I knew the safest place to go was back into the crowded restaurant. But I'd have to run past him to get there. So I turned and started to jog to the corner. Behind me, I heard the hooded man pick up his pace, sneakers slapping the sidewalk.

He's coming after me.

I turned the corner, glancing both ways. No sign of Colin. No taxis. No one on the sidewalk. A scrawny black cat darted between parked cars and shot across the street.

I started to run full speed now.

Was the hooded guy still chasing after me? Yes. Running slow and steady, as if he knew he had me.

The paved sidewalk gave way to a walkway of

wooden planks. My eyes caught the temporary ply-wood wall beside me. Ground Zero. I was running beside the burial ground for thousands of people, running next to the spot where the towers had come down and the people inside . . .

"Colin? Colin?" His name escaped my throat in a shrill, desperate cry.

Where is he? Did he really leave me down here?

My shoes clonked on the wooden walkway as I ran, gasping for breath. No one around. No one to help me. Running along the side of the deep hole, the enormous graveyard. I heard car horns blaring, but so far away, a million miles away.

The wind picked up again with a low howl, blowing hot against my face. I spun away. I squeezed between two parked cars and darted like the black cat to the other side of the street. Too close. I'd been standing too close to all that death.

My chest heaving, I glanced back. "Ohhh." A low moan escaped my throat as I saw him trotting slowly, steadily toward me. The hood covered his face. He raised one hand. And in the yellow glare of a street-lamp, I saw a dark, slender object in his hand.

A knife? No. I squinted hard as he moved closer. A box cutter?

Oh God.

I spun away, turned to run, and my heel caught—jammed in a grate. I twisted my foot and let out a cry as wrenching pain shot up my leg. I tumbled forward, hit the pavement hard.

Panic swept through my body as I struggled to pull myself up.

Footsteps thudded the pavement behind me.

Before I could move, strong hands grabbed my shoulders.

"No—!" I screamed. "Please—not my face! Not my face!"

28

To my shock, the hands released me. I whirled around.

"Huh? *You?*" I whispered. "What are *you* doing here?"

Tommy Foster took a step back, his eyes locked on mine. He wore a tight-fitting, white dress shirt, half-untucked from black denim jeans. Beads of sweat had formed along his thinning hairline. I could smell the sour aroma of beer on his breath.

"Tommy, what are you doing here?" I forced the words out, still struggling to catch my breath.

"Did I scare you? I'm sorry." He held his hands awkwardly out at his sides, as if he didn't know what to do with them. He had stains on both shirt cuffs.

"S-Someone was chasing me," I stammered. "Did you see him? Where did he go? He was right behind me. He . . . he had a box cutter, Tommy. He—" The words caught in my throat.

Tommy frowned and glanced over my shoulder. "I didn't see anyone. Are you sure?"

I swallowed. My throat ached from my scream. "A man in a dark hood."

Tommy shook his head. "No. I came around the corner, and I saw you running. I didn't see anyone else." He helped me to my feet.

"I don't understand. He was right behind me. I was so terrified. I couldn't see his face. But I saw the thing in his hand."

Tommy shook his head. "I'm sorry. Good thing I showed up, huh? I must have scared him away."

I stared at Tommy, still trying to catch my breath. "Yeah. Good thing. You . . . you may have saved my life. Why are you down here?"

"I drew Lindy duty tonight," he said, with a crooked smile. "My other guys are off on other cases. Saturday night. Busy night. So I'm your guy tonight."

I began walking slowly back toward the restaurant, the only place where there was light and people. The heel on my shoe wobbled a little, but at least I could walk on it.

"How's it going with Colin?"

I shrugged. "It's hard, Tommy. Hard to act normal. I always told my dad I'd be a lousy actress."

"Any clues? Anything?"

"Not really."

"Maybe he's a better actor than you are," Tommy said, kicking a beer can off the sidewalk into the curb.

"Were you at the movies with Colin and me?"

"No. I've seen it." He brushed sweat off his forehead with one hand. "Listen, I did backgrounds on all three guys. *Four* guys, I mean. Lou D'Amici, too. They all checked out okay."

"Well . . . is that good news or bad?"

"Beats me." Sometimes Tommy looked like one of those cartoon bloodhounds, all drooping jowls and mournful eyes.

"I'm all confused, Tommy. Did you follow me to tell me that?"

He narrowed his eyes at me. "No. I'm shadowing you, Lindy. I want to catch this creep. Sooner rather than later."

"But, Tommy, listen—"

He raised a hand. "Don't say anything. I feel I . . . well . . . I owe it to Ben to . . . you know . . . kinda look after you."

Was he blushing or was it just the lights from the restaurant window?

"Well, thank you," I said. "I'm happy you're on the case, Tommy. It makes me feel a lot safer. How will I be able to repay you?"

"Repay me? I'm doing my job, you know. But . . . well . . . maybe you'll have dinner with me some night."

Whoa.

Is Tommy interested in me?

I didn't have time to think about it. The restaurant door swung open, and Colin came walking out.

"Colin—where were you?"

"Lindy, I'm sorry. Have you been out here long? I

told the waiter how much we enjoyed dinner, and he dragged me into the kitchen to meet the chef. They wouldn't let me out of there."

I turned to Tommy. How would I ever explain him to Colin? But Tommy was already hurrying away, ducking his head low, so Colin wouldn't see his face, I guessed.

Colin pointed. "Who was that?"

"Just a guy asking directions," I lied. "He was looking for a bar on West Broadway."

Colin snickered. "He's got a long walk." He slid his hand casually over my shoulder. "Let's find a taxi. I'll take you home." He smiled, bringing his face close to mine. "Unless you've changed your mind about coming to my apartment?"

He didn't give me a chance to answer. He pressed his mouth against mine and kissed me. He wrapped his arms around me, held me tightly, and we kissed in the bleeding red light from the window.

"Not tonight," I whispered. "Sorry. Not tonight."

Please, don't let it be Colin. Please . . .

But in my heart, I knew he was the one.

29

She says her name is Ellen. Is anyone really named Ellen anymore? It doesn't matter. She's hot.

Yes, I was out with another hottie last night.

Lindy . . . Lindy . . .

No way I'm going to let Lindy get away. Once I hook them, I know how to keep my little fishies on the line.

And now here I am in Ellen's sparkling, little town house apartment, all white—the walls, the couch, the shag rug in front of the couch—just right for *shagging*? Ha ha.

We're on the low, white couch, making out like two horny teenagers who've never had sex before. We were sitting up, but now I'm on my back and Ellen is on top of me, kissing me like crazy with hot, wet lips, her tongue checking to make sure I have my back molars, her hands playing with my hair, sending chills to the back of my neck.

Wow.

I'm like ready to come in my pants, and she won't quit. I hardly know the girl. I met her after work at J.J.'s, the little bar tucked in between the two enormous skyscrapers on Third Avenue. She said she was a something-or-other at Bloomingdale's. I didn't hear. I was probably studying her tits. Nice ones. The black tube top she was wearing didn't leave much to the imagination.

I think she liked me right from the beginning. Or maybe she was just horny. She kept grabbing my arm and touching my chest, laughing at every dumb joke I made, pressing her head against my shoulder as she laughed. A clear invitation, right?

I knew I was in—even before dinner.

She had dark red lipstick on her full lips, a dimple in one cheek, black eyes that caught the light, all sparkly. She wore her straight, black hair tied in a French braid behind her back. And what else can I tell you? It was lust at first sight.

I let her drag me home after dinner. We both knew what we wanted to do to each other. Yeah, I had fun with Lindy last night. But tonight I knew I was ready for a workout. You're only young once, right?

We're still lip-locked as we make our way to her bedroom. Also white! White walls, white bedspread, white wall-to-wall carpeting, a bleached blond-wood dresser . . . What is this girl's problem? Did someone at Bloomingdale's tell her white was chic?

I check out the room over her shoulder. She won't let go of me. I have to peel her off me to get undressed. I pull off my shoes and toss them across the white carpet. I can barely stand up, I've got a hard-on the size of Cleveland.

She's suddenly got music on. I don't know where it's coming from.

No. Oh, please no. Barry Manilow.

Strike one, right?

Ellen has disappeared into the bathroom. I search around for the stereo to turn that wimp off, but I can't find it.

Okay. Whatever. I can deal with Barry Manilow. This girl is so hot, we could do it to Gregorian chants.

I tear off the rest of my clothes and throw them in a heap, pull back the white bedspread, and pile into bed. And *ta-da*—there she is, emerging from the bathroom wearing nothing but a red-lipped smile. And *what* a body.

Oh man, am I ready for her!

Her hair falls over her face as she slides toward me on the bed, and I—

I—

Ohh, I feel sick.

She's untied her braid. She's let her hair loose.

And as she turns out the bed table light, it's Mom. Yes. Mom's hair falling over her face, in shadow now but I can still see it and remember it. Her hair always too long and parted in the middle, hanging straight down like witches' hair. Mom was too old to have such long hair, all ratty and tangled. Like her brain.

Oh, Ellen.

Your hair is too long and too free.

I grab it in both hands and pull her face to mine. I kiss her hard, too hard maybe. She lets out a little cry. I keep my grip on her hair even though it makes me sick. Sick and angry.

Ellen, why did you untie it? Why did you do this to me?

Oh yes. I fuck her. But it isn't right. It isn't what I wanted. She moans and moves with me, head tossed back, long, black hair spread over the pillow like a puddle of spilled ink.

I shut my eyes and fuck her. I have to shut my eyes. Her hair is alive like a million snakes.

Eyes shut, I see each hair curling, coiling, writhing around her face, a million snakes.

I remember your hair, Mom. Does that surprise you? Does it surprise you that it still disgusts me?

I come with a soft groan, ease myself out of her quickly, and open my eyes.

The hair is all I can see. It glistens with sweat now, still fanned out on the pillow. Still breathing hard, she smiles and reaches for me, wiggling her finger.

But I raise my arm and drive my elbow hard into her larynx.

A choked whistle escapes her throat. Like the last bit of air going out of a balloon.

Her eyes bulge. She can't breathe. I drive my elbow into her throat again, and I hear something crack.

Her whole body jerks up, knees rising, arms shooting out. A reflex, I guess.

I cry out as her hair begins to move. It lifts off from the pillow, flying straight up around her face, reaching up, the long snakes reaching for me, wanting to pull me down, down, down to her face. Her face tilted at a strange angle now, eyes shut.

Is she breathing?

I don't think so.

But her hair still rises up, whipping at me, slapping at me, wrapping around my wrists, trying to grab me. What can I do about her hair?

I jump out of bed. I'm off-balance, for some reason. I glance back and see the hair standing straight up, waving in the air like black wheat.

I have to deal with it.

I find a pair of scissors in a sewing drawer. I click the scissors as I return to the bed, click them open and shut as if sharpening them.

I'm excited.

I can deal with the hair now. I have to deal with it. I can't let it stand up like that. I can't let it grab me and coil around me.

I remember this hair with such dread, such embarrassment. Mom, you are too old to leave your hair this long.

Snip, snip.

The problem is easy to solve. Why is my hand trembling? I grab Ellen's head, hold on to it to steady myself, and then continue cutting. Snip, snip. I'm cutting close to her scalp. I'm making it nice and short.

It doesn't take long. Why am I breathing so hard? It's really hard to catch my breath. I guess it's just the excitement.

When I'm finished, I toss the scissors onto the bed. I'm holding long, thick strands of her hair in each hand. It's lifeless now, like Ellen, dead and limp and oily. It doesn't wave or whip around or try to grab me.

Yes, a victory. The hair is mine. But what can I do with it? I can't leave it here. I can't carry it around.

Sometimes ideas just flash into your mind when you need them. Gripping the hair in my hands, I cross the room to Ellen's desk. I find a large, manila mailing envelope. Yes, perfect. I stuff the hair into the envelope. It makes a nice bulge. I try to flatten it.

It's a gummed, self-sticking envelope. I pull off the strip of paper and seal the envelope tight.

Very good. Very good.

Now what?

I jump as behind me, Ellen lets out a loud burp. Just air escaping.

You're dead. Leave me alone, Ellen. I'm still dealing with your hair.

Now what? Now what?

Oh, yes. I'm good under pressure.

Here is Ellen's address book. A flat, green leather book with lined pages. Her handwriting is neat and tiny.

I pick out a page at random. I run my finger down it, then stop at a name. Katie Marvin. Must be one of Ellen's friends. She lives in Quincy, Massachusetts. Excellent.

I tear out the page from the address book. I find a pen

in the desk drawer. My hand trembles as I address the envelope. Katie Marvin . . . Quincy, MA. Katie, you'll receive a nice surprise in the mail.

Tomorrow I'll be sending you a souvenir of your old friend Ellen.

30

I hurried to work Monday morning and got there an hour early because there was a *FurryBear* manuscript I was supposed to read for Saralynn. Rita was reading it first, and I asked her to make a copy for me so I could take it home over the weekend. But, of course, Rita forgot.

So now here I was at 8:45 on a Monday morning searching Rita's desk for it. *FurryBear's Big Toothache,* one of those books that teach kids not to be afraid to go to the dentist.

No. Not on Rita's desk. Did she deliberately hide it so I couldn't read it on time? My best guess was that she took the only copy home with her on Friday to make sure she had read it and I hadn't.

I was always dreaming up conspiracies where Rita was concerned. And I was usually right.

I accidentally bumped the mouse on Rita's computer, and the monitor flared to life. I watched as it came into focus—a cosmetic surgery Web site. Lots of face photos, befores and afters.

Apparently, Rita had neglected to go offline before she went home on Friday. Was she planning to have some work done? She was my age, maybe even younger. Why would an attractive girl of twenty-three or twenty-four, with dozens of men after her, be thinking of cosmetic surgery? Was Rita more insecure than I imagined? Or more vain?

I straightened her stack of manuscripts and, sighing, returned to my cubicle. I really didn't want to think about Rita. She was a total bitch, and I was praying for the day when I saw her hurrying out on her lunch break with a résumé in her hand, sneaking off to a job interview somewhere else.

Would I celebrate the day Rita left? Does a bird have lips?

I took a sip of the latte I'd bought at the Starbucks next to our office building and thought about my bird series. It wasn't going well. So far, I hadn't been able to find the right authors.

I turned to my computer and pulled up the four summaries of the books I was supposed to do. I squinted at the screen, but my mind went to Colin and Saturday night.

He could see I was shaken when he took me home. I couldn't stop thinking about the guy in the hood, the guy who'd chased me down that dark, frightening street and then disappeared when Tommy appeared.

It couldn't have been Colin. Colin said he was inside the restaurant, talking with the chef. And why would

Colin put on a hood, hide his face, and come after me like that? He had no reason to frighten me.

It had to be Jack or Brad, I decided. Unhappy that I was out with Colin. Did that make sense? Not much.

Sitting in the cubicle, running this through my mind, I started to shake. My teeth chattered. I had to fight back the tears.

There was poor Ann-Marie, her arm sliced up and down, unable to lose the paralyzing headaches. All because of me. And now some creep in a hood was coming after me to . . . to . . . slice me, too? To *kill* me?

Get it together. Get it together. A few weeks from now, life will be normal. Peaceful. And maybe Colin and I . . . Colin and I . . .

The phone rang. I glanced at the clock. The office wasn't even open yet. Who would be calling? I pushed line one and picked up the phone. "FurryBear Press. This is Lindy."

"Lindy, hi. You're there."

"Who is this? Jack?"

"Yeah. It's me. How's it going?"

"Jack, I didn't think you had my office number."

"I'm a good detective. You busy for lunch? I'm going to be in your neighborhood."

A long pause here.

I was still trembling, still feeling shaky. *Don't say no. Keep saying yes.*

"Okay," I said. "Why don't I meet you in front of my building."

I have to call Tommy, I thought. Make sure he has someone watching us.

Jack started telling me about these important meetings he had in the city this morning. Saralynn came in. She glanced into my cubicle, saw that I was on a personal call, and strode quickly to her office.

I could feel my face grow hot. Why couldn't Saralynn come in and see me working? Why did she have to see me sitting here talking to Jack?

It took awhile to get off the phone with Jack, but I finally managed it. "I don't want to have lunch with you," I muttered. "I want you to go away and never come back."

Rita strolled in and saw me talking to myself. She offered me a cheery "Hiya." I watched her unpack a Starbucks cappuccino and a jelly doughnut. "How do you get away with that?" I asked. "You're skinny as a rail."

"It's a *skim* milk cappuccino," she replied. I couldn't tell if she was kidding or not.

Saralynn called the two of us into her office for our weekly Monday morning meeting. She cleared away a stack of files, and we sat down at the round glass table in the corner of her office by the window. A wonderful view. I stared out at the Empire State Building and the Chrysler building, gleaming in the morning sunlight.

A giant stuffed FurryBear sat on one end of her green leather couch, a permanent guest. Framed book covers covered the wall behind the couch, a very colorful display. FurryBear had won a Nickelodeon Kids' Choice Award as Book Series of the Year, and the trophy—a bright orange blimp—stood prominently on Saralynn's glass-top desk.

Saralynn passed out a printed agenda for the meeting. There were only three of us, but she wanted to show how efficient she is. "Lindy, any authors on board for our lovely bird series?"

Ouch. "Well, no. I'm having lunch with a woman tomorrow. She's from the Natural History Museum and she says she has a lot of contacts."

Frowning, Saralynn shuffled through her folder of schedules.

"I know I'm a little late signing up authors—" I started.

Rita jumped in. "Lindy asked me to help her find some people and I have three or four who might work."

Saralynn's frown disappeared. "Oh, that's good, Rita." She set down the schedules.

Rita turned to me. "I'll give you the list when we're through here."

"Thanks," I said weakly.

I'd bet a million dollars Rita didn't have a list.

"Well, follow up on that, Lindy," Saralynn said, making a check mark next to that item on her agenda. "Let's not get too far behind. We don't want to make our friends at Grosset nervous before we even begin."

"Uh-huh," I offered, thinking of a dozen ways I could murder Rita.

"Number two on the list today," Saralynn said, pressing the top of her pen to her lips. "The *FurryBear* toothache manuscript. Have you both read it?"

"Well, no—" I said.

"Yes. I had a few problems with it," Rita said, sliding the manuscript out of her bag and setting it down on the table.

Saralynn had her eyes on me, an accusing stare. "It's only twenty pages long. You didn't have time to read it?"

"It's not that," I said, feeling my cheeks go red again. Should I rat on Rita? Why not! "I asked Rita to make a copy for me on Friday afternoon, and I guess she forgot."

Saralynn pointed the pen toward me. "And you didn't remind her?"

"Well—"

"Did you ask me for a copy?" Rita looking all wide-eyed and innocent now. "I'm so sorry, Lindy. I didn't hear you."

Should I punch her in the face? Should I just reach across the table and punch her so hard she'll *need* cosmetic surgery?

"Maybe if you're not too busy," Saralynn said pointedly to me, "you could read it today. It doesn't go to the copy editor till tomorrow."

"Oh. Fine. Good." I knew I was blushing, blushing from anger. What could I do about it?

That's pretty much how the whole meeting went. Rita just knows how to play Saralynn, and I don't have a clue. I do twice as much work as Rita. In fact, I usually end up doing half of *her* work. But somehow she gets twice as much credit and praise, and manages to make me look like a pathetic loser at the same time.

Saralynn stood up and crossed the office to her desk, which meant the meeting was over. Rita turned to me at the door. "I'll get that list of authors for you," she said with a sickly sweet smile. "I hope it helps you out of your jam."

"Great," I said through gritted teeth. I started to follow her out the office door, but Saralynn put a hand on my shoulder, holding me back. She waited till Rita was back in her cubicle.

"This is a very small office, Lindy," she said in a low, steady voice, her silvery eyes locked on mine. "You really have to try harder to get along with Rita. She's only trying to help you."

Oh, wow.

Not my morning. Rita wins big-time.

I nodded and slunk away like a wounded bird. Should I be thinking of ways to kill myself instead of Rita? Maybe throw myself on my letter opener?

Rita had that same sickly sweet smile on her face as I passed her cubicle. Had she overheard Saralynn?

"Do you have that author list for me?" I asked, my voice trembling.

She shrugged. "Must have left it at home this morning. I was in such a rush. I'll bring it tomorrow."

My hands were balled into tight fists. I could feel the anger well up in my chest.

I turned—and let out a startled gasp. "Brill! Don't sneak up on me like that."

His eyes went wide behind his Buddy Holly glasses. "Sorry." He was very dapper in a charcoal pinstriped suit, a pale blue dress shirt, and a bright red-and-white-polka-dot bow tie. Brill is the only one who dresses up for the office, and I'm sure he thinks the rest of us are total slobs.

"Someone called for you," he said. "While you were in with Saralynn. It was kinda strange. It came to my phone. The person was whispering. I could barely hear. I put it through to your voice mail."

"I wonder if someone's sick," I said. My heart started to pound. A whispered phone message? I thanked Brill and hurried to my cubicle.

I could see Rita's eyes on me. I picked up the phone and pressed the MESSAGE key. After a few seconds, I heard the whispered voice, a fake, strained whisper that sent chills down my back:

"Saturday night was fun, Lindy. Just keep saying yes."

Ohmigod! Saturday night?

Colin.

31

So a kid came up to FurryBear at a stage show. I think it was at the Ohio State Fair. And when FurryBear reached down to hug the boy, the kid grabbed his nose and pulled it off."

Brad tapped out his cigarette. "This was a guy in a costume, right? You don't really believe in FurryBear, do you?"

"Yes. Of course it was a guy in a costume. But this was in front of about ten thousand people. So Furry-Bear took back the nose from the little boy, and he held it up in both hands, and he blew on it really hard. And he said, 'Always remember to blow your nose, kids.'"

Brad uttered a weak laugh. "Ha ha. Funny."

I shrugged. "I thought it was funny. Guess you had to be there."

He gave me his crooked grin. "Got any more Furry-Bear stories?"

"No. I'll save them for another time. Oh. Well. There was one time when there was a screwup, and *two*

FurryBears showed up at the same mall. And they got into a fight—"

"Yeah. Save it for another time," Brad said. I think he was teasing me, but he said it with a kind of scowl.

Yes, Saturday night and I was out with Brad Fisher. The charade continued. Yes, lunch with Jack Smith. Yes, drinks with Colin on Thursday night. Yes, Brad Fisher on Saturday. And still no results from Tommy Foster and the police.

"I can't keep doing this," I told Tommy over the phone after seeing Colin on Thursday night. "I'm going crazy. How could I sit there and act like everything was okay with Colin? He could see I was a nervous nut."

"Calm down," Tommy said. "Take a breath. We're gonna catch this guy. We're getting close, Lindy."

"Getting close? How?"

"I'm on it," Tommy said. I could hear him tapping keys on his computer. "I'm on it like white on rice."

"I hate that expression," I snapped.

I suddenly began to think Tommy was acting like a jerk. Someone was threatening my life. They'd been in my apartment. They knew where I worked. They attacked my roommate. And he sat there typing while he talked to me, only half listening.

And what kind of advice was he giving? Why should I keep saying yes to these guys when one of them could be a homicidal maniac?

"I'm on it like *brown* on rice," he said.

"Tommy, are you making jokes? If you think this is funny, I'm just going to hang up."

His tone changed. "I don't think it's funny, Lindy. That's why I took the case myself."

"It's not a case. It's my *life*!"

"I'm keeping an eye on Colin O'Connor, okay? I told you I did a profile on him. He checks out okay. But I won't rely on that. I know it's hard, but you have to chill a bit. You sound really stressed."

"You—you want me to chill?" I stammered. "And to keep saying yes to these guys?"

"Not for much longer. The guy will give himself away, Lindy. And when he does, I'll have someone there. I promise."

"I don't know how much longer . . . ," I started. I suddenly pictured Colin's apartment, Colin making love to me, groaning softly as he moved above me. He was so gentle . . . so loving.

I had slept with him. And now he planned to *kill* me!

That was Thursday night. Later, Shelly called, and I was actually glad to hear from him. He was as intense as ever, making jokes, telling me about a horrible-but-hilarious conversation he'd had with his mother, who really did sound like a total nutcase.

Shelly sensed that I was down, and without asking why, he worked hard to cheer me up. "I heard that sigh," he said. "What's up with you, Lindy? You seem distracted."

"Just work," I said. I couldn't bring myself to confide the truth. Sure, I needed someone I could talk to about everything, but I had Ann-Marie and Luisa for that. They had both been so understanding and kind. Why bring Shelly into it?

I met Shelly for a quick lunch near my office on Friday. He had a million funny stories. I barely got a word in. But I knew I could relax with him. I didn't need a police escort.

After lunch, I startled myself by backing him against the front wall of the restaurant, and I kissed him, more passionately than I'd planned. I guess I was just so grateful to be with someone I didn't have to suspect.

Saturday night. A warm, windy night, the air heavy and wet, making my hair droop and my skin feel all spongey. Brad and I were walking toward the pier at the South Street Seaport at the bottom of Manhattan.

The Seaport is a touristy area of several blocks. Seafood restaurants, a big fish market, mall-type stores—an Abercrombie and a J. Crew—a few large, noisy bars—very yuppy places. It's where the Wall Street financial guys and girls come after work to pump some beers, let off steam, and hook up.

Brad led the way to the long, wooden pier that stretches out into the river. Spotlights played off three tall-masted sailing ships bobbing in the low waves. Seagulls squawked somewhere in the distance. Couples walked arm-in-arm. A pretzel seller leaned over his cart and coughed, a loud, hacking smoker's cough.

The wind picked up, salty-smelling, kind of sour, fluttering my hair. The wooden planks squeaked under our feet. Brad slid his arm around my shoulders. "Let's take a look at this schooner. I love old sailing ships."

I stopped at the bottom of the sloping gangplank. A shiver rolled down my back. I turned and glanced down the pier. Where was Tommy's guy? I didn't see anyone who looked like a cop. But Tommy had promised someone would be watching my every move.

Brad narrowed his little bird eyes at me. "What's wrong?"

"Uh . . . nothing," I said. "Thought I saw someone I know."

I held back. I really didn't want to walk out on this narrow pier with Brad without one of Tommy's guys nearby.

Brad motioned to the old schooner, sails flapping noisily in the wind. "I love the water," he said. With that beak of a nose and those round, black eyes, he really did look like a seagull. "I'm a Coney Island boy myself. I think I told you that last time. I grew up on the beach. Mom said she had me in the water when I was two weeks old."

"Cute," I said. "Can a baby float at two weeks?"

He grinned. "I don't remember."

We turned and started back toward solid land. My heartbeats started to return to normal. I still didn't see anyone watching us.

"Check it out," Brad said. He had stopped at a break in the pier railing and was pointing down at the water. "Those fish glow in the dark. Wow. You can see them so well at night."

I didn't want to stop. I wanted to keep walking, off

the pier, away from the water. But I turned and gazed down into the dark waves, far below. Through the oily, black murk, I saw a faint, green glow.

And then I felt a sharp pain in my back.

Someone had pushed me. Pushed me hard. I tumbled forward.

I shot my arms out and grabbed for the rail. Missed.

And, hands flailing, too startled to scream, I plunged over the side.

32

I heard someone scream—but the scream cut off as I hit the water. Facedown. A belly flop that sent pain shooting over my body. I shut my eyes as the freezing water surged over my head.

Cold panic swept over me.

I can't move my arms. My legs. I can't move.

The water—it's pulling me down.

I could feel myself sinking deeper. The current beneath the pier pulled me hard to the left, then pushed me to the right, helpless, like a clump of seaweed.

My chest ached. The shock of the cold seemed to paralyze me.

Move, Lindy—move.

With a great effort, I kicked my legs. Arched my back. My shoes suddenly heavy as rocks. But I forced myself to move. I *willed* myself up.

You're drowning. You're going to drown now.

You've always known you were going to die in the water.

No.

Ohmigod no.

I had to fight my own thoughts.

I opened my eyes. At first, I saw only darkness. Thick and black. But then I stared into a green glow, so close I felt I could reach out and touch it. Glowing, green fish—lighting my way?

Lighting my way to the other side?

Didn't people always see a glowing light just before they died?

I crashed over the surface of the water and gulped in deep breaths of air. My hands thrashed the cold water. I kicked hard.

Calm. Calm. Take steady strokes, Lindy.

You're breathing now. Someone will pull you out.

Brad, where are you? Are you going to jump in and save me?

Or did you push me?

My whole body shivered. The current was carrying me away from shore.

Is anyone looking for me?

Is anyone coming? Brad? Where are you?

I lowered my head and swam hard. I can do this. I'm not going to drown under this dock. No way.

With a shuddering gasp, I reached out both hands and grabbed on to a wooden piling. My hands slid right off. The thick log was slimy, slippery with green, mossy weeds slick as gelatin. The current pulled me away. Frantically thrashing the water, I pulled myself forward again.

I sucked in a long breath, my lungs aching, and made

another grab. This time, I held on—and wrapped my arms around the slimy log.

Pressing my body against it, I raised my eyes to the dock. Bright white light blinded me. I gasped and lowered my gaze. I heard shouts up above. Someone called my name. Brad?

Brad? Did you push me?

It had to be you. Did you try to kill me?

No. It didn't make sense.

I didn't say no to you, Brad. I thought we were having a nice time. Are you just a sick, twisted fuck? Did you bring me out on this pier to kill me, you bastard?

My fear quickly turned to anger. The anger helped me fight the river current, helped me hold on to the moss-slick piling although my arms were numb from the cold.

"They're coming!" someone shouted from the dock. The bright light washed over me. "Hold on! They're coming!"

I heard the low roar of a boat motor behind me.

You're safe, Lindy, I told myself.

For now.

"Here. Put this on." Brad held up a Seaport sweatshirt he'd run to buy at a shop near the pier. He helped slide it over my head. "This will help you stop shivering."

When they raised me onto the dock, he rushed forward and hugged me. His face was all concern. He pulled weeds from my hair and ran to buy a tall cup of coffee.

Nice acting job, I thought.

Two police officers, both looking about fourteen, with close-shaved blond hair and narrowed blue eyes, waited patiently for Brad to pull the sweatshirt over me. One of them, lanky and thin as a rail, kept sniffing, studying me suspiciously. Did I smell bad? The other cop already had a beer belly, his uniform shirt pulled tight over his stomach.

These weren't Tommy's guys. Where was my police protection tonight?

The coffee burned my throat. It started to warm me. Brad wanted to hold me against him, but I backed away.

We were standing in the entrance of a small book-store across from the dock. The store was closed but the windows were brightly lit. I read the title of a Stephen King novel in the window.

Just what the world needs. More horror.

"What happened, Miss Sampson?" the tall, lanky officer asked, eyes studying me.

"I don't know. I didn't see. Someone pushed me."

I turned to Brad. I couldn't read his expression. His mouth hung open slightly. He was breathing hard.

"Were you depressed? Did you jump?"

"No way!" I shouted. "Are you crazy?" My voice trembled.

"We have to ask," the other cop said softly.

Brad finally spoke up. "Someone shoved her. I didn't get a good look at him. I was so . . . stunned."

The two cops turned to Brad. "Are you and Miss Sampson . . . ?"

"We . . . we were out together," Brad fumbled for words. "You know. A date."

"Did you have a fight?"

Shivering, I tightened my arms around myself. The sweatshirt was soaked through now and wasn't keeping me very warm. Water dripped from my hair, down my forehead. I just wanted to get home and into some dry clothes and . . . away from Brad.

"No. No fight," Brad said, almost in a whisper. He pulled a pack of Camel Reds from his pocket. He offered the pack to me. I shook my head. He knows I don't smoke. "A man ran up behind Lindy. I didn't see his face. He wore a hood. I think it was black. It was . . . you know . . . a hoodie. He had it pulled over his face."

A man in a hood? The same man who followed me outside the restaurant downtown last week? Brad must be telling the truth. He didn't know about the hooded man last week.

Unless *Brad* was the hooded man?

I decided not to say anything. These cops weren't going to be helpful. I needed to talk to Tommy.

I searched the area around the dock. Stores were closed. People were leaving the bars and restaurants, heading home.

"You didn't see his face?" the lanky cop asked.

Brad shook his head. He lit his cigarette with a red plastic lighter. "I already told you."

"Describe him."

Brad took a deep drag on the cigarette. "Kinda average. Not too tall. Maybe a little shorter than me. I'm not sure. It happened so fast. Not fat or anything. I think he wore black pants, kinda baggy."

Like the guy last Saturday night . . .

The chubby cop turned to me. "Did he steal your bag? Was it a robbery?"

I blinked. My bag? I had brought a large, soft canvas bag.

"Here it is." Brad picked it up from the pavement. "It flew off her hand when she went over the side. It landed on the edge of the dock. I picked it up." Brad handed it to me. He had a strange smile on his face, as if he had just scored a point or something.

I shivered harder. "Listen, I really have to get home," I told them. "Can you guys give me a lift?"

I didn't want to go home with Brad. Maybe he was telling the truth about the hooded guy. But I had to get away from him. I had to get warm and dry. I had to think.

Someone had tried to kill me.

How could I keep it together now? What are you supposed to do after someone tries to kill you?

"We're almost finished," the lanky officer said, staring at his notepad. "We'll take you home. Unless . . ." He turned to Brad.

"I don't have a car. We came on the subway," Brad said. "I could get us a taxi."

"Please take me home," I told the officer.

Brad took another drag on his cigarette and didn't react to that.

"So it wasn't a robbery attempt," the chubby cop

said, keeping his eyes locked on mine. "Maybe it was just a psycho. He saw you at the gap in the railing and made his big move."

"I . . . I'm really cold," I said, my voice quivering along with my body. I touched my hair. Sopping wet. I tried to dry it a little with a sweatshirt sleeve.

"We'll take your info in the car and get back in touch. We have a regular patrol at the Seaport. Maybe we'll spot the guy wearing the black hood." He motioned for me to follow them.

Hugging myself, I started toward the squad car in the parking lot. Brad hurried after me. He wrapped his arms around me. "Jesus, I don't know what to say. I'm really sorry, Lindy. I promise we'll have a . . . dry time next time."

Next time?

"We won't even drink anything," Brad said, still holding me.

Someone tried to kill me, and he's making jokes.

"I . . . I'm sorry, too," I murmured. Why did I say that? Maybe I was in shock a little bit?

He pressed his face against mine but didn't try to kiss me.

You didn't push me, did you, Brad? It really was a guy in a black hoodie, right?

I swung out of his grip and hurried after the two officers.

"Anyone home?" I slammed the door behind me and bolted it. "Ann-Marie? Luisa? Are you here?"

Silence.

I glanced at the neon Budweiser clock over the mantel (a gift from Lou). Eleven o'clock on a Saturday night. Of course no one was home.

"I need to talk to somebody!" I shouted to an empty apartment.

I grabbed my cell out of my bag. I'll call Ann-Marie, I thought. She must be out with Lou somewhere. She'll come home when I tell her what happened.

No. Wait. What am I thinking? I have to get changed first. I have to warm up. I'm not thinking clearly. My brain is all crazed.

Lindy, hello. Take it one step at a time.

I took a long, hot shower. I let the steam swirl around me, so soft and comforting. Then I pulled on my softest sweatpants and sweatshirt and thick, woolly ski socks.

Yes!

I felt a little better. Now what?

I didn't have time to decide. The phone rang. I hurried across the room and lifted it to my ear. Was it Ann-Marie? I really needed to talk to her. Was it Tommy Foster?

"Hello?"

"Lindy. I just took a chance. I thought maybe you might be hanging out at home tonight."

"Shelly? Well, hi. What are you doing?"

I was happy to hear his voice. Shelly could cheer me up. Could I confide in him? Tell him what happened to me tonight?

Yes, I decided. Yes, I could confide in Shelly.

"I'm watching paint dry," Shelly said. "It's totally exciting."

I dropped onto the edge of my bed. "You're joking. What's going on?"

"I'm not joking. They painted my apartment today. I'm watching paint dry."

I laughed. "Well . . . are you high on paint fumes?"

"I'm high on life. Are you . . . uh . . . alone there? You just hanging out? I mean . . . you want to meet or something?"

"Come over, Shelly. I have some wine in the fridge. Maybe we'll get trashed or something."

"Or something? Are you trying to get me into bed?"

"Shut up. I'd really like to talk. I had a kind of frightening thing happen tonight."

"Okay. Talk and wine. I'm there."

"Thanks. I mean, hurry over, okay?"

I didn't want to be alone. I needed to talk about everything with someone. Ann-Marie was so involved with Lou, so totally obsessed. We were still close, but it was harder to get through to her. Especially since I told her about Lou coming on to me. That kind of changed things between us. I could see it in her eyes. A distance that was never there before.

Shelly was funny and nice. Yes, he could get intense, but of all the guys I'd been seeing, he was the only one I could confide in.

I went to the mirror, brushed my still-wet hair, and pulled it back tight into a blue scrunchie. I was spreading lip gloss on my lips when the phone rang again.

"Hello?"

Silence.

"Hello?"

Hard, noisy breathing.

I let out a gasp. "Stop it—please!"

Raspy throat sounds. The breathing came faster.

"Stop calling me!"

My heart pounding, I clicked off the phone and threw it across the room.

Why do I do that?

Lindy is such a nice girl. And I think she really likes me.

Why do I call her and breathe and groan like that? Am I a sicko? I don't even find it that thrilling.

You're such a bad boy, Shelly. Why do you keep calling her?

Okay, it's a little exciting. Admit it. You love to hear that intake of breath she makes when she realizes it's the breather again.

You like to hear her shout at you.

You're bad, Shelly. You have to stop.

You have to be nice to her. You like Lindy. You like her a lot.

Now put down the phone and get over to her apartment. She's waiting for you.

PART FIVE

33

Dune Road in Westhampton stretches through a narrow strip of sandy ground, with the ocean on one side and Peconic Bay on the other. Houses on stilts, all windows and light wood and weather-graying shingle, rise up on the yellow sand on the ocean side. The houses are pressed close together, as if huddling against the powerful waves. Some of them tilt into the wind off the ocean. Frothy water from high-tide waves washes under the stilts of houses built close to the shoreline.

Sand blows over the narrow, two-lane road that separates the beach houses from the bay-side houses. Every year, the ocean beach grows a little narrower. As it erodes, the houses find themselves more vulnerable, closer to the powerful waves that steadily crash onshore.

The houses on the bay side of Dune Road are more modest. Many of them are just bungalows, clapboard cabins and shingled, one-or-two-bedroom shacks built as summer rentals. The houses sit lower to the ground, many of them surrounded by tall grasses and reeds, swaying in the ocean winds.

The backs of the houses face the gentle, saltwater bay. Sometimes the bay is flat as a lake. Sometimes low waves splash on the grassy shore. No one swims in the bay here. The water is much too shallow. You'd have to walk for miles before the water came up to your knees.

Westhampton is the first Hampton town you come to when you drive out on the Long Island Expressway from the city. It is the youngest and flashiest and sluttiest and least snooty of the Hamptons. Westhampton has more young people jammed into share-houses, more dance clubs, more bars, more silver and gold beach jewelry and thong bikinis, more Beamers, more people my age desperate to hook up, to find a summer romance.

I know I sound like Lindy, the travel guide. But you have to understand, I've been coming out to the Hamptons all my life. Usually to visit friends, because my parents could never afford a place out here.

Sometimes when I was little, we'd wake up at dawn and drive out just for the day. Mom would pack a big cooler of sandwiches and canned sodas for lunch. We'd change our clothes out of the back of our old station wagon and spend the whole day on one of the ocean beaches, Hotdog Beach in Hampton Bays, or Cooper Beach in Southampton on those rare occasions when my parents wanted to spread their beach blanket near the rich and beautiful.

Sunburned and yawning, we'd have dinner at a dinky little drive-in called Slo-Jim's on Montauk Highway that Dad said had "the best clam rolls on Long Island." Then we'd make the long drive back to the city and arrive home after ten o'clock, exhausted, sandy, and happy.

Those sunny days in the Hamptons formed some of my happiest family memories. And I couldn't help remembering them in great, slow detail as Lou drove my two roommates and me to the summer house Luisa had found for us on Westhampton Beach.

This was supposed to be an escape for me, for all of us. But of course I couldn't leave my problems behind.

What a shame I couldn't summon up the joy and expectation I had felt when I was a kid. Now, I had to fight back my feelings of dread, my thoughts about the killer I had attracted on the Internet.

Ann-Marie sat in the front passenger seat of the SUV, complaining most of the way about Lou's driving. He was one of those guys who thought it was a sport to dart from lane to lane, cutting off other cars, then speeding up to tailgate the next car, forcing it to change lanes and make room for him.

I slumped low in the backseat beside Luisa and wished Lou wouldn't turn driving into some kind of macho test. Once in a while, I could see his face in the rearview mirror. I could see his eyes on me and the biggest leering grin. I hoped I was imagining things.

"Lou, give us a break," Ann-Marie pleaded, as he cut sharply to the right in front of an enormous Shell oil truck.

He slid his right arm around her shoulders and held the wheel with his left. "Hey, you've been on my case the whole trip. I thought you were crazy about me."

"I never drove with you before. You're starting to lose your appeal."

She was serious, but it made him laugh for some reason. Ann-Marie hadn't said a kind word to him the whole trip. In fact, she'd seemed angry from the time he picked us up, which I thought kind of strange. Lou was doing us a favor, after all. Driving us two-and-a-half hours out to our beach house.

I tried to change the subject. I turned to Luisa. She wore black tights and an oversized black T-shirt with a white spiderweb down the front. She had a blue and gold Florida Marlins cap pulled down over her straight black hair.

"Where'd you get that hat?" I asked. "You're not a Marlins fan."

She pulled off the cap and examined it. "Someone left it in the bar. I thought it was kind of kitschy."

"It's so awesome that your cousin found us a place right on the beach," I said. "A house we can actually afford."

"See? It's all who you know," Lou chimed in.

"Actually, I had to be very very nice to him," Luisa said with a sly grin. "If you know what I mean."

Ann-Marie gasped. Lou and I laughed. "You said he was your cousin," Ann-Marie said.

"A distant cousin," Luisa replied, spinning the cap on her finger.

"You've been watching too many reruns of *Sex and the City*," I said. "People don't really act like that."

Luisa rolled her eyes. "Right."

"I can't wait to see Goth Girl with a suntan," Ann-Marie said.

"Neither can I," Lou said. "And in a thong bikini!"

Ann-Marie punched him on the shoulder. "Shut up."

Luisa leaned forward, wrapping her hands around Lou's throat. "Lou, how funny are you? *Not!*"

"Hey—let me drive!" he protested.

Somehow we made it to Westhampton, and found the little red clapboard house on the bay side of Dune Road. We loved it immediately.

A short gravel driveway led past a white picket fence to the side of the house. Two flower beds bursting with bright red and purple impatiens framed the front walk.

The house was small and hot and damp inside. I hurried to open windows and let some fresh air in. Then I glanced around, trying to take it all in. One large, high-ceilinged room downstairs, kitchen, diningroom, livingroom all in one, a lot of knotty pine paneling, lots of wicker furniture, a square dinette table at the back window looking out to the bay, an enormous silvery blue swordfish mounted over the mantel.

Lou plopped down on the only armchair, an ugly brown thing with a recliner head and footrest. "This is a great make-out chair. Who wants to sit on my lap?"

Ann-Marie shook her head. "I'm warning you, Lou . . ."

Ann-Marie pulled Luisa and me away to explore the

rest of the house. "Come on. He's being a total pig for some reason."

A short hall, also knotty pine with framed sepia-toned photos of the lighthouse at Montauk Point lining the walls, led to a downstairs bedroom. Very nice. Walls painted a creamy off-white, filmy, white curtains at the sides of a large window with a cushioned window seat to gaze out at the sunset over the sparkling bay.

Sliding glass doors led to a private flagstone terrace. Painted wrought-iron table and chairs . . . a small-sized Weber barbecue grill, rust forming on one side of the lid . . .

"We need a pool back here," Ann-Marie told Luisa, shielding her eyes from the lowering, red sun. "Why don't you talk to your cousin about it?"

"Too close to the bay," I said. "I don't think a pool is allowed."

"Look." Luisa pointed. "What is that?"

I followed her gaze. A hummingbird buzzed over a clump of tall grass. "Haven't you ever seen a hummingbird before?"

Luisa shook her head. The three of us stared at the tiny creature as it hovered over some wildflowers at the edge of the terrace, bumping the blossoms gently, its wings a blur.

"Wow, that's so cool," Luisa said. "Aren't hummingbirds supposed to be good luck?"

My cell phone rang. My breath caught in my throat. "I hope so," I said.

34

Jack Smith called and said he'd really like to see me when I got back to the city. I wanted to tell him I was *never* coming back, that I'd decided to move to Westhampton and become a clam digger.

Would he believe that?

I don't think so.

I had no desire to see Jack. I wanted to say, "Jack, buy one of those plastic, inflatable girls. She'll think you're fascinating." But even after my dip in the river, Tommy Foster insisted I keep saying yes. So I said, "Yes, of course. Let's get together," in my sweetest voice. And I told him to call me Monday after work.

Honest truth: I was afraid of Jack, too. He was just too ordinary, too uninteresting. Sometimes I was sure it had to be an act. Like he was controlling himself. Like he was keeping his real self deep inside, afraid to let it come out.

Because he knew he was evil.

Two weeks had passed since my terrifying plunge into the Hudson River with Brad looking on. I had nightmares about it every night. In two of them, I drowned.

Ann-Marie said if you die in your dreams, you're supposed to die in real life. She said she learned that in a psych class.

How helpful was that?

Ann-Marie hadn't forgiven me for accusing Lou that night. It was such a mistake. What was I thinking? It put such a dent in our friendship. I wondered if we could ever patch it up and be really close again.

Since Ann-Marie seemed so distant, I started confiding more in Shelly. We had dinner two or three times at Good Enough To Eat, a comfortable, down-home restaurant on Amsterdam Avenue in my neighborhood, where they serve up enormous portions of meatloaf and fried chicken with old-fashioned mashed potatoes and gravy.

Shelly insisted we finish off our dinners with big slices of coconut cake, and I told Shelly the main result of all the horror I was going through was that I was going to put on twenty pounds.

"Lindy, you'd still look hot if you put on *fifty* pounds," he said.

Sweet.

Then, of course, Shelly jumped up from the table, puffed out his stomach, and did an imitation of me walking around with an extra fifty pounds. He had everyone in the restaurant laughing, even though they didn't know why.

Shelly loved to perform. Sometimes I found it hard to

get him to stop, to be silent, to sit still and stay in one place, to stop his mind from jumping from topic to topic.

But once I did, he was a terrific listener. He stared at me, giving me all of his attention. He held my hand. He was kind and sympathetic and tried to assure me that the whole thing would soon be over.

A real friend.

I tried to be a friend to him, too. I begged him to let me see some of his writing, but he always said no, he wasn't ready to share it. I begged him to at least tell me what it was about. He said he was trying to work out a murder mystery, but he was having trouble with it. The plot wasn't coming along.

"Why a murder mystery?" I asked.

He shrugged. "Why not?" The only time he really clammed up was when I asked about his writing.

He often held my hand and, once in a taxi, he slid his arm around my shoulders and pulled me close. He'd come hang out at my apartment sometimes after our dinners. But he never invited me to his apartment. We kissed but it never led to anything more.

Shelly never made a move.

I puzzled over that. Was he gay? I didn't think so. Was he really shy? Was he being considerate, knowing all the trouble I was in, waiting for me to make the first move?

A real mystery. And actually, I was relieved. I really did want Shelly as a friend. I'd realized I wasn't attracted to him in a sexual way.

And now it was Saturday night, escape night for me, and here I was in the glamorous Hamptons. A hundred miles away from the city.

Ann-Marie and Lou had driven into town and come back with an enormous picnic basket filled with clams and mussels and shrimp and lobster salad and corn bread and coleslaw, bottles of white wine, and a key lime pie for dessert.

It was a warm night, balmy for June, with warm breezes off the ocean, and a fat, full moon to light the beach. We spread a blanket on the sand, dropped down around it, and had our fabulous picnic dinner, the first of the season.

"It doesn't get any better than this!" Ann-Marie declared. And we all raised a glass to that and agreed with cheers and laughter.

But I glimpsed the scars on Ann-Marie's arm as she raised her glass, and I felt a chill that kept me from laughing and joining in.

Here I was in this beautiful setting with my friends a hundred miles from New York City. I loved the silver moonlight splashing over the waves. The feel of the evening-cool sand beneath my legs. The fresh, fishy smell of the air off the ocean.

But those scars on her arm . . .

I couldn't escape by running away.

"Check out that house." Lou pointed to a beach house behind us near Dune Road. "It's all glass. You can see everyone inside it!"

The house was a basic A-frame, on low stilts, but the side facing us—facing the ocean—was nearly all glass. Several of the rooms, upstairs and down, were brightly lit. Squinting hard, I could see people sitting around a table in the kitchen, having dinner. A man and a woman, both in swimsuits, lingered in one of the bedrooms.

"Wow. You know what they say about people in glass houses," Luisa said. "They should buy curtains."

"Think if we stay late, we can see them fucking?" Lou asked.

"Why don't you wait here and see," Ann-Marie said, still on his case.

Three guys came wandering out from another beach house, and Luisa invited them to join us for pie and wine. Then a couple sat down on the sand near us. The woman was tall and pretty with straight black hair down her back. I thought I recognized her from Stuyvesant High, but maybe I was wrong.

Some twelve-packs of Budweiser magically appeared. Someone had a boom box cranked up high. More people joined the circle. Two big dogs wrestled onto our blanket. Ann-Marie and I struggled to pick up the remaining food before it got crunched.

And suddenly it was a regular beach party.

I started talking with the woman with the sleek, black hair—and she *was* the one from Stuyvesant. Jeri Waldberg. She was in the class after mine. I remembered her because she'd been a tremendous actress. She starred in all the school plays, and there were rumors that Hal Prinee was her uncle and was going to put her in a big musical.

I guess the rumors weren't true. She told me she was marketing assistant at a small boutique ad agency in SoHo. When I told her I worked at FurryBear Press, she said it sounded like real fun. She should only know.

A small campfire blazed, sending tall flames licking up against the purple night sky. The music grew louder, and a few couples began to dance. In the flickering fire-light, I saw Luisa dancing with a bare-chested guy in baggy cargo shorts, his hair down to his shoulders, his arms covered with tattoos. They both carried cans of beer as they danced. Her head was tossed back as if frozen in laughter.

I was wearing a pale pink midriff top and low-riding jean shorts, and I began to feel the chill of the night air off the ocean. I shouted to Ann-Marie that I was going to run back to the house to get a sweatshirt. Standing with a group of people near the fire, she waved, but I'm not sure she heard me.

I pulled on my plastic flip-flops and ran to the road, hugging my bare shoulders. A Westhampton police cruiser was stopped at the edge of the sand. The two cops inside had their windows rolled down and were watching the party. I could hear the beeps and static from their police radio.

I gave them a wave as I crossed Dune Road in front of them. They both waved back. "How's it going?" one of them called, but I kept running.

I unlatched the gate on the picket fence and started up the walk to the front door. The flowers along the walk swayed in the gusting wind. The full moon had faded behind a thin veil of low clouds. The porch light glowed brightly. Lights were on inside the house. Curtains fluttered in the open front window.

I reached for the front door—and it opened. I gasped in surprise. "Lou—"

"Hey, Lindy. How's it going?" I smelled beer on his breath. His skin looked yellow under the porch light. He smiled. "We've got to stop meeting like this."

I faked a laugh and tried to slide past him. "Just getting a sweatshirt."

He blocked my way. "You look totally great," he said. His eyes moved up and down me. "No offense, but I like it when you show some skin."

I groaned. "Give me a break, Lou."

He grabbed my wrist. "Why don't you give *me* a break, Lindy? You know how I feel about you."

"No. Come on." I tried to snap my hand free, but he held on tightly and forced me closer to him.

"Jus' lissen to me." He was slurring his words. "That's all. Jus' lissen, okay?"

"Let go of me. Now."

He released my wrist. He lowered his face to mine. His eyes grew wide and sad. "You know I'm crazy about you. You know I'm tired of Ann-Marie. I can't stop thinking about you, Lindy."

"Stop it," I insisted, keeping my voice low and steady. I tried to hide my fear. But he was so much bigger than me; if he decided to make a move, it would be hard to fight him off. "Isn't this a rerun?" I asked. "Didn't we already have this conversation?"

"You're totally beautiful," he said. He ran his fingers through my hair.

"Stop it, Lou. I'll call the police. Really. See that cop car out there?" I turned. The cruiser was gone.

"You're the most beautiful woman I've ever seen," he said. "I just want to touch your hair. Your face." He ran his fingers down my cheek. I started to tremble.

Should I kick him in the balls and run?

What about Ann-Marie? If I told her this happened again, would she believe me?

"Lissen to me. Jus' lissen. When I'm with Ann-Marie, I always think of you. Really. I always picture you."

"Stop it!" I screamed. "I don't want to hear that. Ann-Marie is my friend. Do you understand that? You can't tell me things like that. Don't you understand—"

"Every time I'm with her," he repeated, nodding his head. "I see you there. I pretend it's you. But I don't want to pretend. Get it? I stay with Ann-Marie so I can be close to you. But I don't want—"

"Shut up. Just shut up. You know what I've been going through. Don't you care that someone attacked Ann-Marie? That someone tried to kill me? Don't you care at all?"

No reply. He grabbed me by the shoulders. He spun me around and backed me against the front door. He was breathing hard, his chest rising up and down beneath his muscle shirt. His eyes locked on mine. I could see he was trying to decide what to do next.

"Lou, please," I whispered.

He held me by the shoulders. His hands were sweaty. His fingers dug into my skin.

"Lou, listen to me. Let go—*now*."

He slid one hand down over my breast. "Nice," he whispered.

"Lou—?"

I'm going to knee him, I decided. I'm not going to stand here and let him rape me. I'm going to knee him in the balls, then run. And I'm going to tell Ann-Marie the truth—no matter what the consequences.

"Lindy . . ." he whispered, his hand still caressing my breast. "Lindy . . ."

I took a deep breath. Clenched my muscles.

"Hey, guys! What's up?"

At the sound of Ann-Marie's voice, Lou let go of me and lurched back. His mouth dropped open and his eyes went wide for just a second. But he recovered quickly and turned to face Ann-Marie with a smile. "How's it goin', babe?"

Ann-Marie's eyes were on me. I'm sure she could see that I wasn't okay. I couldn't recover as quickly as Lou.

"What are you doing here, Lou?" Ann-Marie asked sharply.

He shrugged. "Had to use the potty." He motioned to me. "The front door was locked, so I was helping Lindy get inside." His thick, black eyebrows rose up on his forehead. He stared at me as if challenging me to contradict him.

Ann-Marie studied me for a long moment. "Are you having a fun time tonight?" she asked.

I didn't say a thing.

She wrapped her arm in Lou's. "Let's go back to the party, baby."

Did she see Lou feeling me up? How long had she been there?

How much did she hear?

35

This one was wrong from the beginning. I think her name was Evan Something. Yeah, she had a boy's name. She looked not great, kinda browned-out and mousey, and no lipstick or anything, her face all one color, and her eyes a sick green. Not at all like her picture on the Web site.

I took one look at her and knew she was a loser. I took her to a movie so I wouldn't have to talk to her.

Just my luck, she was one of those women who likes to giggle and chat and whisper stupid comments all through the movie. And I hated the way she shoved popcorn into her mouth, not delicate at all, but shoveling in handful after handful like someone was going to steal the bucket from her.

Then when she finished the whole tub, she tried to hold hands with me. With the butter and salt still fresh on her skin. I thought I would blow chunks. She wouldn't even let me concentrate on the movie, she had so many "witty" things to say.

I knew there was no way I could sit through a meal

with her. And when we walked out of the theater and I saw the two greasy popcorn kernels stuck to her stringy, brown hair, I knew she had to die as soon as possible.

I mean, what kind of person lets her hair dip into her food? Girls named Evan, I guess. I mean, you start out life ten steps behind if you're a girl and your parents call you Evan, for Chrissakes.

I suppose I should have felt sorry for her. But I couldn't. She put herself on the Internet for everyone to see and judge. If she had any sense at all, she'd forget the whole dating thing, stay in her apartment, turn on the Lifetime channel, and have a good cry.

That would have been safer, at least, than going out with me. Tricking me with that glamorous photo and then walking around with buttery popcorn waste matter in her hair. Because now I had to kill her.

"Who Murdered Evan?" That's the name of *this* story.

I took her to the service area at the side of my apartment building. It's a narrow walkway, a dark space a couple yards wide between my building and the one next to it, where the garbage cans are hauled out and where all the delivery guys go. I'd checked it out before. I'd always known it would come in handy.

It's very dark there at night. And if you go halfway back, no one can see you from the street.

So I invited Evan to my place. Told her I'd cook us a quick, romantic dinner. You should have seen her eyes light up when I made that suggestion. She licked her lips with the fattest tongue I've ever seen on a human.

Oh God. Is this a night to forget?

I could have been with Lindy. Instead, I picked an Evan.

Evan help me! Ha ha!

I took her around to the side of the building. I told her I had a private entrance at the back. She didn't even hesitate, just followed me down the narrow walkway.

Near the back, I turned to face her. I could hear the roar of air conditioners all the way up the side of the building. I heard pigeons squawking from a roost on a low window ledge.

Then it was Evan's turn to squawk.

She smiled because she thought I was going to kiss her. Her lips parted. I grabbed her head and slammed it as hard as I could into the brick wall.

"Hey!" she shouted. Her eyes clamped shut with the pain.

I slammed her head into the bricks one more time, just to get her attention. Her head tilted to one side. Her legs gave way, and she collapsed to the sidewalk.

I wrapped my hands around her throat and choked her. Harder. Harder.

The eyes didn't pop. I love it in the cartoons when the eyes pop. But it's harder to achieve in real life.

I squeezed until my hands hurt too much to continue. I knew Evan was dead, but I always like to give it a little extra.

I dragged Evan to the back of the passageway. I turned her on her stomach so I wouldn't have to see that ugly face, all twisted in pain, mouth frozen open, that fat tongue hanging out like the thumb on a catcher's mitt.

Bye, Evan. It's been great.

Shaking my sore hands to make the pain go away, I started toward the front of the building. I was nearly to the street when I saw the flash of blond hair.

A flash of color. A red skirt and a white top. And that silky, blond hair bobbing behind that beautiful face as she hurried away.

She was running away.

I recognized Lindy. And I'm sure she recognized me. Oh no. Oh God, no.

Was it really Lindy? Did she see the whole thing?

Please, no. I like her so much. She's the first girl I ever really liked in this way. Lindy is so perfect. So perfect in every way.

Oh, please no.

I'm heartbroken. There's no other word for it. I'll never be the same. I know that. I'll never be able to forget her.

Lindy—why? Why did it have to be you? Why did you have to be there watching me with Evan?

Shit! Pull yourself together, dude. You know what you have to do now.

Game over. Sign Off time. Delete delete delete.

Go do it. Kill Lindy now.

36

Friday night, Ann-Marie pulled up to the building in a rented, white Toyota Camry. Luisa and I tossed our weekend bags into the trunk and climbed inside, Luisa stretching out sideways on the backseat, me sliding beside Ann-Marie and struggling with the seat belt.

"Where's Lou?" Luisa asked. "What's with this rental car?"

Ann-Marie bit her bottom lip and stared straight ahead at the windshield. "Lou is history," she said. "He's a loser."

Thank God, I thought. I wanted to jump for joy.

Instead, I put a hand on Ann-Marie's shoulder. "What happened?"

She frowned and pulled away from the curb. "I'm going up Amsterdam to 125th," she announced. "We'll take the Triboro, I think."

"What about Lou?" Luisa persisted.

"Nothing about Lou," Ann-Marie said. "We weren't getting along. That's all. It's been building for a long time."

I wanted to tell her what a rat Lou was. I wanted to tell her what the son of a bitch tried to do to me. The disgusting things he said. I wanted to assure Ann-Marie she'd made the right decision. Good riddance to a big heap of garbage.

But I knew better than to put my two cents in. In my junior year at NYU, another really close friend of mine broke up with a guy I knew had been cheating on her. I made the mistake of telling her how smart she was to lose the guy, what a total piece of shit he was.

The next day they got back together, and neither of them ever spoke to me again.

So I made sympathetic noises and tried to change the subject. But Luisa, leaning forward with her elbows on the back of my seat, was relentless as ever. "How did you dump him, Annie? What did you say to him? Did you break his heart? Come on, tell us. Did you make the big guy cry?"

Ann-Marie shook her head in reply, and I saw a teardrop slide down one cheek. "Grow up," she told Luisa. That's all she said. And it closed the subject for the rest of the ride to the Hamptons.

It started to rain as soon as we exited the LIE. The forecast was for rain the whole weekend and, for once, the weather guys got it right.

Saturday morning was dreary, with rain pouring down on the tall grass behind our house, thunder low in the distance, and the fog so thick we couldn't even see the bay. Dune Road was empty. I guessed a lot of people had seen the forecast and decided to stay home this weekend.

I didn't mind it that much. I like rain. I liked the sound of it pattering on the roof of our little house. A cozy fire would have been perfect, but we didn't have any firewood. The lights flickered once or twice, but the power stayed on.

Ann-Marie, wearing a long-sleeved, red-and-white-striped shirt over a one-piece swimsuit, paced back and forth for a while, nursing a mug of coffee. "What are we doing out here?" she asked, staring out the water-smeared window.

"Relaxing," I said.

Ann-Marie sighed and slumped into a chair away from the window with a romance paperback. She'd brought a stack of them out. She said she likes them because she can read one a day, and they all have happy endings.

Wow. That wasn't a good sign. I hoped she wasn't heading into one of her depressions. I'd been through them with her, and they weren't pretty.

After lunch, a guy Luisa had met on the beach last weekend picked her up in his BMW convertible. She disappeared with him, saying, "Don't wait up." Sort of a joke between us. Luisa says that every time she goes out.

The rain had stopped but the fog still hung low, clinging to the tall grass in back. Water poured from the gutter at the side of the window.

"Want to take a drive or something?" I asked Ann-Marie. "Go into town and look around?"

"Gee, that would kill ten minutes," Ann-Marie said, not looking up from her paperback. "There's nothing to see in Westhampton."

"How about a movie?"

Why did I feel I had to entertain her? I guess I felt bad for her because she had given up a guy she'd been crazy about. She was going through a hard time and didn't want to share it, the way she always had in the past. She wouldn't even talk about Lou, which wasn't like her at all.

"Let me see what's playing." I reached for the *Dan's* paper, the local Hamptons weekly. But before I could open it, my cell phone rang. I ran across the room and grabbed it off the table. "Hello?"

"Hey, Lindy, it's Brad."

My breath caught in my throat. "Brad? Where are you?"

"I'm in the Hamptons, too. I'm staying with a friend. The parents have a house in Quogue."

How did Brad know I was in the Hamptons?

"Crummy day, huh?" I said.

"Well, the rain stopped. You doing anything? I'd really like to see you." He was talking rapidly. He sounded nervous.

"I don't know. Ann-Marie and I . . ."

"I'd really like to talk to you, Lindy. It's kind of important."

Staring out at the fog, I suddenly felt chilled. I knew Brad was waiting for an answer, but I didn't know what to say.

I didn't have any police protection out here. This was supposed to be my place to escape from everything.

"You know Magic's Pub?" he asked. "On Main Street in Westhampton. It's a little bar with great hamburgers. I'm there now. Think you could meet me?"

He's not going to try anything in a restaurant, I decided. "Okay," I said.

I clicked off the phone and turned to Ann-Marie. "Brad. Says he has something to tell me."

Ann-Marie looked up from her book. She tsk-tsked.

"Come with me," I said. "Get dressed and come into town with me. I'd feel a lot safer."

She thought about it, then shook her head. "I'm not up to seeing people today. I don't want to sit in a bar with you and Brad and talk about how the weather sucks and when is summer really going to start."

"I know you're in a bad mood, but you won't come as a favor?"

She shook her head again and pulled the shirt tighter around her swimsuit. "You'll be okay. Don't get alone with him." She returned to her book.

Sighing, I changed into an oversized maroon sweatshirt, which I pulled down over a pair of gray leggings, tugged a floppy faded denim cap over my hair, borrowed the car, and splashed over the rutted Dune Road to town.

I found Brad hunched over the tiny bar at Magic's Pub, cigarette dangling from his mouth, a half-empty beer glass between his hands. He pulled the cigarette from his mouth when he saw me and flashed his lopsided grin.

He was wearing a striped Polo shirt and khaki cargo shorts. His white hightops were caked with sand. My great detective skills told me he'd been walking on the beach.

"Hey, Lin, nice to see you." He jumped down from the bar stool and kissed me on the cheek. His beaky, broken nose bumped my ear. I wondered how he moved his nose out of the way when he seriously kissed women.

My mind was skipping around, noticing every detail, alert. He ordered me a Coors. We took our beers to a square, wooden table in the corner. He complimented my hat and told me how awesome I looked three or four times. He kept tapping one hand on the tabletop as we talked. I don't think he realized it.

He seemed almost as tense as me, which is saying something.

What did we talk about? I didn't really listen. Brad was talking really fast, gesturing with both hands. I could tell he'd had a few beers while he was waiting for me.

There was enough tension at our table to blow up the restaurant, I thought. I was actually relieved when Brad suggested we take a walk.

The fog hovering low over the ground made the little

town look surreal, like in a black-and-white movie. The air felt heavy, hot and steamy.

"A short walk on the beach?" Brad suggested. "We're almost there. I jogged in the rain this morning, and it was really eerie and beautiful at the same time, so much fog you could only see a few feet out."

I pulled back. I didn't want to be alone with him on a deserted beach. "I don't think so," I said.

"Oh, come on. A short walk," Brad insisted. He took my arm and practically pulled me toward the beach. "You've got to see it. It's amazing."

"Was . . . anyone else there?" I asked, struggling to hide my fear.

"Oh, sure. Lots of people. It was actually crowded."

Tall, gray waves crashed onto the sand. The fog was so thick on the shoreline, the waves seemed to appear from out of nowhere, leaping out of the wall of mist. The sky darkened as storm clouds rolled low in the sky.

Brad lied. We were the only ones on the beach.

My mouth suddenly felt dry. My heart started to pound. "It's beautiful, but I really have to go," I said.

Brad didn't reply. His little bird eyes squinted out to the fog over the water. He led us closer to the water.

"Let's go, Brad. I'm getting soaked by the spray," I said, pulling my hat lower on my head. I tried to turn back, but Brad grabbed my arm.

"Hey," I said. I didn't like the expression on his face. His eyes were suddenly wild, and he let the cigarette fall from his mouth, onto the sand. Beads of water covered his forehead and cheeks.

The sky grew darker. Thunder roared somewhere out on the ocean.

"Brad—let go." I pulled back.

But he grabbed my shoulders and held on to me. "Lindy, I didn't want to do this," he said, shouting over a crashing wave. "I really didn't want to do this."

37

I've decided to go back to my old girlfriend."

I stared at him, my heart pounding. "Huh?"

"I don't want to hurt you. I thought I owed it to you to tell you in person. But she and I, we had a good thing going, and we're going to try again."

I know I was supposed to be upset by the big announcement. And I know I should have handled it better, more maturely. But I was so relieved by Brad's news, I burst out laughing.

38

Monday night, I knew it was time to kill Lindy.

I couldn't force my dinner down. I left the pizza slice growing cold on the plate. I was so jumpy, I knocked over my can of Bud and sent suds pouring over the table.

I jumped up, my stomach in a knot, and started to pace the apartment. Ten steps forward, ten steps back. I was so crazed, I counted the steps!

I guess I knew what I had to do. I was just gathering my energy, like a freight train picking up steam, getting it together, getting my *freak* on.

I didn't want to kill Lindy. She was the nicest, most beautiful girl I ever knew. But she had seen me in the alley between the buildings. She saw what I did to that woman named Evan, and then she ran.

And I've been living in terror ever since. Living in a panic, waiting for the front door to burst open and the police to come storming in, guns raised.

I lift my hands in surrender. One of them thinks I'm holding a gun, and he fires once, twice. The first bullet catches me in the head. It makes a large hole in both sides of my skull, and my brains come spraying out the back. The second bullet pierces my heart and blood spurts up.

I end my life as a fountain.

Unless I can get to Lindy before she tells the police what she saw. Unless I kill Lindy first.

You see, my imagination is too good. I can picture exactly what will happen to me. I can see it all so vividly, in THX sound and digital projection.

But I can also picture what will happen to Lindy. Lindy will be dead, and I'll be safe again. I can eat my pepperoni pizza in peace. And I can go back online and find another girl, even hotter than she is.

So, a man's gotta do what a man's gotta do. I can't live in this square box like a mouse in a trap. Ten steps by ten steps.

You can't do that to me, Lindy.

I call her first to make sure she's home. I act romantic and hint about how I hope she's alone. That makes her giggle. And yes, she tells me her roommates are out. "And I'm so glad you called."

Yes, I'm glad I called, too. I'll be even more glad in an hour or less. Of course, I'll miss you, Lindy. I'll think about you often. Maybe even when I'm out with a new hottie, who only wants to do me, do me, do me, and not spy on me when I'm gettin' busy with someone else.

I suddenly felt kinda crazy. Like I wanted to scream at the top of my lungs and punch my fist through the wall. Like I wanted to jump on the table, even with its puddle of spilled beer, kick the pizza slice across the room, leap up and down and crow like a rooster.

I used to be a great crower when I was a kid. Mom always begged me to stop. One day, Dad stopped me by punching me in the mouth. He knocked out three teeth, and I never crowed again.

Get yourself together, Shelly.

This is a sad occasion, remember. You're going to see Lindy for the last time.

I walked uptown to work off some of my extra energy. It was only fifteen or twenty blocks. People turned and looked at me on the street. I could feel their eyes on the back of my neck.

I guess I was talking to myself the whole way. Sometimes I heard what I was saying, but it didn't make any sense to me.

I flexed and unflexed both hands, limbering them up, getting the muscle tone just right. You should always warm up before exercising, right?

"Hey—what are you staring at, lady?" I waved a fist at her. "Like to have your eyes checked for you?"

Ha ha. She turned and ran. Good thing. I can't do two in one night. At least, I've never tried.

I was sweating by the time I reached Lindy's building on Seventy-ninth Street. I wiped my forehead with the sleeve of my T-shirt. Lindy buzzed me in and I straightened my hair in the lobby mirror while I waited for the elevator. A guy's gotta look his best at all times.

She greeted me at the door with a smile. She had her blond hair tied up in a bright blue scrunchie. She wore a loose-fitting blouse and a short, pleated skirt that came down only halfway to her knees. My little cheerleader.

I kissed her and followed her into the livingroom, so shabby and not feminine at all, even though three women lived there. How can they stand all that ugly, clunky used furniture?

"How are you?"

"What a dreary weekend. All that rain."

"You should've seen the fog at the ocean."

And blah blah blah.

All the time, the siren is going off in my head. My own personal wake-up call, saying, "Get this show on the road."

So I stepped up close to her. She stopped talking and smiled. She thought I wanted to kiss her again. I wrapped my hands around her throat, delicately at first. She seemed to like it.

And then I tightened my hands. Tightened them around her smooth, warm throat, holding her still as she struggled, shutting off her air.

She wheezed and honked like a goose. A terrible sound. I knew it would give me nightmares for days. The terrified look in her eyes wouldn't help, either. Lindy, don't look at me like that. It's your own fault, you know.

Honk, honk, honnnnnk.

Her face, that pale, pretty face with the smooth, lus-

trous skin—her face turned bright purple. Like the egg-
plants you see stacked up at Fairway Market on Broadway.

Her face darkened and her hair fell loose and her eyes
stared up at me, blankly now. And the honking stopped,
but I still kept squeezing. Never do a job halfway, right,
Shelly?

I kept squeezing, even though my hands were aching
now. Even though I had to hold her up above the ground
because her legs had given way. I kept my hands
wrapped around her throat, and I squeezed and
squeezed, making lemonade, dude, squeezing those
lemons, squeezing all the juice out.

Goodbye, Lindy. I grabbed her corpse under the
armpits, and dragged her into the bedroom. I slid her
onto her back on the bed with her head propped on the
pillow. I lowered her eyelids and said goodbye.

Oh yes, oh yes.

I walked out of the building whistling to myself.

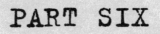

PART SIX

39

Luisa stepped into the apartment, closing the door behind her, greeted by the aroma of stale cigarette smoke. It smells worse than the bar, she thought. Maybe the mayor could do me a favor and ban smoking in here, too!

She had worked all night, busy, lots of guys getting rowdy, amateur beer drinkers, guys hitting on her but no one interesting enough to hook up with. Besides, she felt tired.

I have to find a day job. The night shift isn't as fun as it used to be.

And, I'm not getting *old*—I'm just getting *smart*. Nighttime should be fun time, not, "Can I bring you refills on those Buds?"

She glanced around the livingroom. Didn't anyone ever clean up in here? An open pizza box on the coffee table, a hunk of crust the only remains. Soda cans and beer bottles. Did Lindy and Ann-Marie have a slumber party or something?

"Hey—anyone home?" she shouted.

Silence.

"Lindy? Annie?"

No one home.

What do I want? A shower first, a long, hot shower. And then some clean clothes that don't smell of beer and sweat. And then . . . couch potato time. Maybe I'll lie on the couch and read that stack of *People* magazines and listen to the White Stripes CD I bought three weeks ago and haven't even opened.

Luisa pulled off her top on the way to her room. Her roommates' doors were both closed. It was nice to be alone in the apartment. There'd been so much tension lately, with Ann-Marie dumping Lou, and poor Lindy with the death threats and going out with guys who might want to kill her.

Luisa dropped her bracelets onto her dresser top and pulled off the ivory skull pendant on its chain, then her dangly, plastic earrings. I wouldn't handle it the way Lindy has, she thought. Her cop friend is dumb as a post. I wouldn't say yes to these guys. I'd confront each one of them: "Hey, did you steal my underwear? Did you threaten me?"

I'd be able to tell which one it was by reading their faces.

She keeps risking her life, and it's total bullshit.

Lindy is so nice. Being gorgeous hasn't spoiled her one bit. She's a great roommate and I guess a good friend, even though we don't have much in common. She doesn't deserve all this crap. I wish I could help her.

Luisa pulled off her short denim skirt, slit on one

side. She walked to the bathroom and turned on the shower. She was standing naked except for her patterned, black tights when the phone rang.

Who would call during the day?

She hurried to the phone in the livingroom. "Hello?"

"Hey, Lindy?"

"No. It's Luisa."

"Is she there? This is Brill. From her office."

"Oh, yeah. Hi. Isn't she there?"

"No. She didn't come into work today."

"Really? Weird."

"We haven't heard from her or anything. So we were a little worried."

"Well, no. I haven't seen her. You know . . . maybe she went to visit her dad. He hasn't been doing too well."

"But wouldn't she call in first?"

"Beats me. Listen, I've got a shower running. Can I take a message?"

"Sure. Just ask her to call Brill, okay? Thanks, Luisa."

Luisa hung up and scribbled *"Call Brill "* on a yellow notepad beside the phone. She tore off a sheet and carried it to Lindy's room. She could hear the shower and saw a cloud of steam floating out of the bathroom.

I'll put it on her pillow.

She swung open Lindy's bedroom door and stepped inside. The shades were up and bright sunlight invaded the room. Hot in here, she thought. And everything glowed brightly as if under a spotlight.

Luisa turned to the bed—and let out a startled cry. "Lindy—?"

Lindy lay sprawled on her back on top of the bedcovers, one hand dangling over the side of the double bed, her head at such a strange angle, mouth opened wide.

"Hey, Lindy?" Luisa shouted. A wave of fear rolled down her body. She lurched to the bed and grabbed the dangling arm.

"Lindy? Come on. Wake up. What's wrong? Why are you home? *Lindy?*"

40

I dreamed that someone had grabbed my arm and was pumping it hard, calling my name. I heard myself groan, and I opened my eyes slowly.

Such bright light. I blinked and turned my head away from the window. And saw Luisa hovering over me, holding my hand.

"Ohhhhh." I groaned again and squinted, trying to focus on Luisa. Naked except for a pair of black tights. A blue and pink flower tattoo between her breasts. "Huh? What's up?"

Luisa let out a long sigh. "Lindy, I was worried . . . I . . . uh . . . what are you doing here?"

"Sick, I think," I whispered, my throat aching. "Some kind of stomach thing." I rubbed my stomach. It felt sore. Probably from heaving my guts out all night. "I didn't go to work. I'm just wiped." I started to cough.

"You scared me," Luisa said. "I didn't know you were home. I'll get you some water." She hurried from the room.

I pulled myself up to a sitting position. What a long,

horrible night. Did I get food poisoning? All I had for dinner was a Lean Cuisine and a bowl of vanilla Häagen-Dazs.

My nightshirt felt damp and clung to my back. I pulled it down and stretched my arms above my head. My arms seemed to weigh a hundred pounds each. Get it together, Lindy.

At least I wasn't so damned nauseous.

Luisa returned with a bottle of Poland Spring water. She had put on a sleeveless blue T-shirt over her black tights. "Are you okay?"

I took a long drink of water. The cold felt good against my hot throat. "I think I'm alive," I said.

"Were you out last night?"

"No. I stayed in. I didn't feel sick until I went to bed." I took another long drink.

We chatted for another few minutes, then Luisa left to take a shower. She told me Brill had called, but I really wasn't up to calling the office.

I drifted in and out of sleep for the rest of the day. A little after five, I climbed out of bed, took a long shower, emerged feeling fairly strong and human again. I pulled on jeans and a striped Polo shirt, had a bowl of corn flakes, eating slowly, testing my stomach.

I felt a lot better. It must have been one of those twenty-four-hour things. There was no one else home, and the apartment felt hot and stuffy.

Which explains why I decided to go out for a walk.

And explains why I found myself at Shelly's apartment building a short while later.

I didn't deliberately walk to Shelly's place. I was walking aimlessly, really, just trying to clear my head. It was a gorgeous summer evening, the sky still blue and no humidity at all, a cool breeze blowing down Columbus Avenue. One of those great nights in the city when *everyone* is out on the street, and the outdoor cafés are filled, and it's all like a big block party.

And when I found myself in front of Shelly's building, I decided to give his apartment a try and see if he wanted to grab a bite or something. I was suddenly *starving*! I guess because I'd totally emptied myself out during the night.

I found Shelly's name on the directory and buzzed his apartment—3-G. Before he could buzz back, a woman backed out, pulling a baby stroller. She held the door open for me, and I stepped inside the building. I took the elevator to the third floor, walked down the long, carpeted hall to 3-G, nearly at the end, and—hey—to my surprise Shelly's door was open a crack.

Weird.

I pushed it open a little more, poked my head in, and called, "Shelly? You here?"

No answer.

Why was the door open?

I shouted again. Silence. I peered around the room. No one there.

I stepped inside, blinking, waiting for my eyes to adjust to the dim light.

"Ohmigod—!" A cry escaped my throat as the single room of the studio apartment came into focus.

"Oh no. Oh, please no!"

I pressed my hands against my cheeks—and stared at hands and feet, human heads cut off at the neck. Body parts piled on shelves and tables. Hands and feet, stiff as wood and gray, pale gray, in a heap on the couch. A hunk of blond human hair with a square, paper-thin strip of scalp spread out on the kitchen counter . . .

"Oh no. Ohmigod no."

My legs felt weak. My stomach lurched, the nausea of last night returning. And then my eyes stopped at the image on the refrigerator. And I grabbed the door frame to hold myself up.

And stared at myself.

My photo.

A poster-sized, blown-up photo of my face. Covering the front of the refrigerator. Streams of bright red dripping from my nose and ears. Paint? Blood?

My heart raced. I realized I was holding my breath.

Bloodred streaks painted over my face . . .

I forced my eyes away from the photo. Body parts everywhere . . . so stiff and gray, all the same shade, as if they'd been painted . . . and . . . and my face on the fridge . . .

My whole body shuddered. I turned away from the hideous sight. Lindy, get out. Get out!

I spun around—to find Shelly standing behind me.

He had a strange, tight-lipped smile on his face, and his eyes flashed excitedly.

He blocked the doorway. No way to escape.

"Shelly, please!" I cried.

"Lindy, what a nice surprise."

41

I went down to take out the trash," he said. He stepped into the apartment and closed the door behind him. "I didn't realize I left the door open. Welcome to my cozy little home."

He was speaking calmly, normally, that tight-lipped smile on his face. He had to know that I'd seen his terrifying collection. Did he plan to pretend that everything was normal?

"I . . . have to go," I whispered.

"You just got here."

"I know, but . . ."

"It's dinnertime, isn't it?" he checked his watch. "I was writing all afternoon. Guess I lost track of time. Want to grab something?" He took a step toward me. He kept curling and uncurling his fingers, making tight fists, then releasing them.

"No. I can't," I said, eyeing the door behind him. "I just dropped by to say hi. I can't stay."

His grin grew wider. "Sure you can." He took another step closer.

"No. Really. I promised Ann-Marie . . ." Could he see me trembling?

You're a psycho, Shelly. I thought you were my friend.

Why didn't I guess?

I didn't want it to be you.

"I'll make some herbal tea," he said. "You like peppermint, right? Sit down, Lindy. I'll make some room on the couch."

By clearing away the hands and feet?

He moved closer—and kissed me on the cheek. The kiss made me shudder again. Was he too crazy to notice how terrified I was?

Or was he enjoying it?

I couldn't breathe. I glanced at the clump of blond hair on its strip of scalp. Someone's hair. Someone who *used* to be alive . . .

Shelly moved casually to the sink and picked up the kettle. And I made my move. I lunged for the door. Pulled it open and dove into the hall.

"Hey—!" I heard his startled shout behind me.

I turned and forced myself to run. I didn't wait for the elevator. I grabbed the iron railing and practically leaped down the stairs.

I stopped at the first landing, my heart pounding so hard my chest ached, and listened. Was he coming after me?

Up and down the stairwell, I could hear the roar of air conditioners. Voices in the hall above me. A woman shouting. I sucked in a deep breath. Then I turned and ran the rest of the way, my shoes clanging on the metal stairs.

Please don't follow me. Please don't come after me.

A white-haired old woman leaned on a metal walker at the building exit. I couldn't stop in time. I bumped the walker as I slid past her and bolted out the door.

"Fuck you!" she shouted, in a shrill little girl's voice. "Fuck you!"

I turned and saw her waving a pale fist at me.

Was Shelly right behind her?

I took off down the block, past a stationery store closing for the evening . . . a Gap Kids . . . a Starbucks . . .

Where can I hide? Where can I call the police?

I pulled my cell phone from my bag as I ran, and held it tightly in my fist. My lifeline . . .

I dodged a woman with a double baby stroller and turned the corner, running full speed. Yes. A Korean grocery. I edged past a couple of young women examining the vegetables outside the door. Down the long aisle to the back of the store.

Did Shelly see me? Was he right behind?

I leaned against the shelf, struggling to catch my breath, squinting at my phone, waiting for my eyes to focus. I had Tommy Foster in my cell. I just had to force my fingers to cooperate.

Come on. Come on.

Tears ran down my cheeks, hot against my skin. I hadn't even realized I was crying. I pushed the phone buttons. "Tommy, hi. It's Lindy. Oh, thank God. Yes. I found him, Tommy. He's a murderer. A murderer. I had no idea. But I found him. It's Shelly. Yes, Shelly Olsen. It's him. It's him, Tommy. The mystery is solved."

42

Shelly confessed to murdering six women," Tommy Foster said. He took a long drink from his Corona bottle, studying my reaction the whole while. "He confessed to murdering them and cutting off parts of their bodies."

I shuddered.

The waitress leaned over me, a short, pale-faced girl with spikey purple hair and six tiny rhinestones stuck through her nose. She raised a coffeepot over my cup. "Refill?"

"Sure," I said. I realized I was holding on to the white mug for dear life. I moved my hands away so the girl could pour.

Tommy had called the apartment around four o'clock the next afternoon. "I thought maybe you'd be at work," he said.

"No. I didn't go in. I probably should have," I said, sighing. "So you caught him? Did you arrest him? How come you sound so calm?"

"I need to talk you. Meet me at the Dublin House on Seventy-ninth Street, okay?"

"Yeah. Sure. But you caught him?"

"Lindy, we always get our man."

"And so you need my statement?"

"Not exactly . . ."

"I don't understand. Did Shelly confess to everything?"

"Meet me at the Dublin House. My favorite tavern. I think you'll need a drink or two."

But I only ordered coffee. I didn't really want anything. I just wanted to know why Tommy was acting so mysterious. And I needed to know that Shelly had been locked up.

I'd found Tommy at the end of the long bar, Corona in hand, eyes on the Yankees game on the wall TV. He was wearing a shiny blue sports jacket over an open-collared white shirt and jeans, and he looked more hangdog than ever with at least a day or two of stubble on his long, lined face.

I had to tap him on the shoulder to take his attention away from the game. He wiped beer foam off his mustache with one hand and motioned me to a narrow, wooden booth with the other.

I ordered coffee and leaned across the initials and graffiti carved into the hardwood tabletop. "Please— don't keep me in suspense. What happened?"

Tommy patted me with a hand cold from his beer. "We took your friend Shelly into custody. He was there in his apartment, waiting for us, I guess."

"So he didn't chase after me."

Tommy shook his head. "He didn't put up any kind of struggle. Said he was ready to confess."

Something good must have happened in the baseball game. Two preppy-looking guys at the bar let out a cheer and gave each other a high-five.

Tommy didn't glance back at the TV. He kept his eyes on me. "Shelly confessed to murdering six women."

I gripped the coffee mug. "I . . . could have been number seven. I could be dead."

Tommy shook his head. "I don't think so." He had a smile on his face. What was so funny?

"He told us he met the women on the Internet. You know. Dating Web sites. Like you did. He gave us the names of the women. He even had their addresses. He knew them by heart."

"Knew the addresses by heart?"

Tommy nodded. He signaled to the waitress for another beer. "We checked them out, Lindy. And the women are all alive." He stared at me, waiting for my reaction.

I stared back. He wasn't making any sense. "Tommy, give me a break here. I don't understand."

"The women are all alive. Shelly only murdered them in his imagination."

"You're joking."

He shook his head. "I couldn't be more serious. He's a psycho, all right. But a harmless psycho, as far as we can tell."

"But . . . the body parts?"

"He made those. Carved 'em or something. Some of them came off mannequins."

"But he confessed?"

"Yeah, the poor guy is totally delusional. He lives in a fantasy world. Turns out he has a history of confessing to crimes. Confessed to twelve murders in New Jersey about five years ago. He spent time in a mental hospital there. Did he tell you he's a writer?"

"Yes. I begged him to let me see what he writes, but he never would." My hands were shaking. I clasped them together tightly on the tabletop.

"Well, we found a lot of writing samples when we searched his apartment. They were murder stories. They were all about him murdering some woman and cutting off her hair or her fingers or something." Tommy made a sour face. "Sick stuff. Not even that well written."

I shook my head. I felt dazed. I'd really considered Shelly a friend. I'd *confided* in him! He was so funny, so energetic, so . . . crazy.

Tommy finished his second beer and set the bottle down on the table. "He even wrote a story about murdering *you,* Lindy."

"Oh no," I whispered. "I don't believe it."

"In the story, he strangled you in your apartment, left you on your bed, and went home to find another victim on the Internet."

"Sick," I whispered. I lowered my gaze, picturing Shelly at the dance club, Shelly in my apartment, meeting Shelly for the first time at that bar, thinking he was Colin.

"Yeah, a real sicko," Tommy agreed. "But a murderer only on paper. He never killed anyone. Lucky thing, huh?"

"Well, yeah."

"When we confronted him with the truth, he said he *could* kill if he had to. Then he said he didn't want to kill you. But he had no choice. He said he liked you so much, he'd kill for you—if he hadn't already killed you. What a fucked-up bastard."

"Pardon your French," I said. "Isn't that what cops say after using foul language in front of a woman?"

A weary smile crossed his lips. "Only on TV. But I'm glad to see you're getting your sense of humor back."

I sighed. "I don't think I'll laugh about any of this for a long time, Tommy. Where is Shelly now? He's locked up, right?"

He nodded. "Bellevue. You're safe, Lindy. Hey, you want to grab an early dinner somewhere?"

"No. No thanks," I muttered.

He shrugged his shoulders. "Okay then. Case closed."

He stood up, but something was bothering me. "Tommy, what about my underwear?"

He squinted at me.

"You know. Stolen from my apartment. Did Shelly have it?"

"We didn't find it, Lindy. Buy yourself some new panties."

I squeezed out of the booth. "But don't you think—?" I started.

Tommy turned at the door. "We got the creep, Lindy. Now go have a nice life."

43

That night we celebrated the end of the mystery. Luisa called in sick, and the three of us headed right to the bar at Calle Ocho, a big, noisy, sleek Latin-style restaurant on Columbus Avenue, my favorite restaurant in New York.

We were feeling pretty good after two or three mojitos. "We should do this every night," Luisa said. She laughed. "Maybe I'll quit my job."

"I'm already drunk," Ann-Marie confessed. "Isn't that pathetic? On only two mojitos?"

"Four," I said. "But who's counting?"

"Let's keep right on celebrating in the Hamptons this weekend," I said.

"We should give up men and stick to drinking," Ann-Marie said, stirring the sugarcane stick in her glass. She removed it, licked it, then slid it back and forth in her mouth, moaning in pleasure.

"Gross," Luisa said.

"I've seen worse," Ann-Marie said.

We all laughed and ordered another round.

"I knew it was Shelly all along," Ann-Marie said, taking my hand. "I knew it had to be him. He was so . . . what's the word?"

"Nice?" I said.

"Yeah. Nice."

"You can't solve the mystery after it's already been solved," Luisa told her.

"Well, who did *you* think it was?" Ann-Marie asked.

"The quiet one," Luisa said, without having to think. "Jack? The boring one? It's always the quiet ones, right?"

"I didn't have a clue," I said, shaking my head. "Not a clue. That's what was so frightening."

Ann-Marie took a long sip from her straw. "Well, now you can dump them all."

"Except for Colin," I said. "He may be a keeper."

Luisa frowned at me over her glass. "How can you like someone so straight? He's a stockbroker or something, right?"

"It's the dimple in his chin," Ann-Marie said. "He probably had that done."

"That's sssstupid," I said. Why was the room tilting up and down? "I'm going to that party Thursday night. You know. The business party Colin invited me to. That should be weird."

Ann-Marie squinted at me. "If you're so into him, why don't you invite him to the Hamptons this weekend?"

"I'm not ready for that," I said.

The waitress leaned over us. "Another round?"

"I don't think so," I said.

"Why not?" Ann-Marie said, holding up her empty glass. "It's New Year's, isn't it?"

The waitress stared at her. "In June?"

I bought a new dress for Colin's party, a sleek Donna Karan number, your basic little black dress. It was low-cut in back and came down only to mid-thigh, and with a silvery chain belt, the high-heeled black silk Jimmy Choo pumps I'd bought on sale, a beaded bag I'd borrowed from Ann-Marie, the opal necklace my mother had left me, and my hair in a French braid, I was feeling sexy and elegant.

I could see a lot of eyes on me as I walked with Colin through the crowd of well-dressed people. Come on, I'm used to it, but tonight I felt sophisticated and beautiful, and didn't care if people stared or ogled me. I'm a New Yorker, I thought with some pride, and tonight for a change I'm part of the New York party scene.

I couldn't figure out why Colin was acting so stressed. It was just a crowded, noisy party, after all, and he looked pretty elegant himself in a navy pin-striped suit, a pale blue shirt, and a red Ferragamo tie I recognized from magazine ads.

His wavy hair fell over his forehead, and he had even shaved his dark, stubbly beard close so that his skin was smooth and shiny.

But his hand was too cold and sweaty to hold. And he

kept clearing his throat and smiling an uncomfortable smile at me, patting away perspiration on his forehead even though it was cold inside the museum.

He had picked me up in a black Town Car with a driver and had struggled with small talk as we made our way through evening traffic, across Central Park to the museum. After telling me how awesome I looked three or four times, he started spouting information about the Temple of Dendur, as if he was some kind of tour guide.

Yes, the Temple was built out of sandstone blocks in 15 B.C. in Egypt. And yes, the Aswan Dam caused the waters of the Nile to flood, which meant the Temple would soon be completely submerged. So the Egyptian government gave the Temple to the United States in 1965.

"This is the cool part," Colin said. "They shipped the Temple to the Metropolitan Museum block by block. But the museum had no place to put it. So these ancient blocks sat outside in the grass behind the museum for eleven years until they built a wing to hold it."

Um, hi, Colin. Remember, I went to school in New York City? We used to visit the Temple of Dendur all the time. When I was eleven or twelve, after Mom died, my dad even liked to bring me here. We'd walk around the wading pools filled with pennies, and we'd gaze out the glass walls at the park and the playground across the street. And sometimes we'd walk slowly, circling the Temple and Dad would tell me about the Ancient

Egyptians and how they worshiped and the mystery of how they ever built their amazing buildings.

It was a beautiful room for a party, the long glass wall looking north and the sky so low overhead, the long, white-clothed tables set up on both sides of the Temple with tall platters of shrimp and lobster salad and filet, the waiters carrying champagne flutes on silver trays.

Colin started talking to a group of people, and I had to pull his sleeve to remind him to introduce me to everyone. And then a middle-aged man with a very young woman at his side approached, and Colin introduced me and we chatted about the party for a short while.

"That's my boss," Colin whispered when they'd moved on. I started to say something, but he turned to get us some champagne. We clinked glasses and then tilted them to our mouths.

Colin spilled some champagne down his chin. "Why are you so klutzy tonight?" I asked.

He twisted up his features. "I'm cute when I'm klutzy, don't you think?"

"Kind of," I said, laughing.

"I'm just . . . not my best at parties." Then he whispered in my ear. "I'm better one-on-one." His lips brushed my cheek.

"Well, just relax. Everyone seems so nice."

He rolled his eyes. "You don't have to work with them."

"Have some more champagne," I said. "That'll put you in a better mood. I'm going to the ladies' room."

I handed him my champagne flute and made my way through the crowd. I had to ask a museum guard where the ladies' room was. He pointed down a long corridor that stretched through part of the Egyptian wing. I found it easily at the end of the hall. No one else was there. I took a little time to straighten my hair and redo my pale lip gloss.

A minute later, I thought I was returning through the same hallway, but I must have made a wrong turn. I stopped and listened. No. I couldn't hear the party from here.

I turned to go back. Where did I make my wrong turn?

There were no guards to ask. I followed the hall into a vast display room; dimly lit cases revealed vases and pottery parts, carved cats staring out at me from behind the glass with blank eyes, graceful pitchers, a sculpted bird, pale yellow, with its head down, wings raised, ready to attack.

Squinting in the dark, I nearly bumped into a giant stone sarcophagus. Was there a mummy inside? I didn't want to see. Why couldn't I hear the party from here?

I stared at the sculpted bird, frozen in midair, its beak open, anticipating its prey. On the far wall, I saw a dimly lit, red and white EXIT sign.

I was nearly to the open doorway when I heard a cough behind me and the soft scrape of footsteps on the carpet. I spun around. No one there.

Strange. I listened hard. No. No one.

I turned back to the exit, and clutching my little beaded bag, took a few steps—and heard a harsh, whispered cry:

"Lindy, don't say no. Don't ever say no to me."

44

I gasped. "Colin—is that you?"

No answer. I heard footsteps behind me, rapid now.

I glanced back. Too dark to see. The bird in its lighted case stared out at me, wings raised, body arched to attack.

I turned and ran into the wide corridor. I blinked in the bright light, the orange walls a blur.

"Don't ever run from me!" a raspy whisper from close behind.

My heels clonked the hard floor as I tried to run in them.

"Don't run, Lindy. I'll fuck you up. I'll fuck you up bad if you run from me!"

"NO—!" I screamed. "Colin? Is that *you*?"

I let out a cry as a stab of sharp pain shot through my head, my body. Stunned, I staggered back.

A glass case. I'd crashed headfirst into an empty glass case. Dizzy now, I stumbled off my heels. Fell to the floor. Head spinning. Waves of pain rolling over my forehead, down the back of my neck.

I shut my eyes and willed away the pain. And when I opened them, Colin stood over me, breathing hard, sweat making his forehead and his dark cheeks glow. Colin held me tightly, almost fiercely, by the arms, eyes locked on mine. "Are you okay? Lindy, are you okay?"

And then I lost it. I jerked my arms free. "Colin? Was it you?" My voice shrill and angry. "It had to be you. But—why? Why did you chase me?"

And then I remembered our dinner downtown near Ground Zero. I was chased that night, chased for blocks down those dark, empty streets. And then when I'd escaped from my pursuer, Colin reappeared, acting innocent and concerned.

"Why did you want to scare me? Why did it have to be you, Colin?"

He stepped back, arms tensed at his sides. I could see other people behind him, streaming out from the Temple room, eager to see what the commotion was. "Lindy, just sit down, okay? I think you've had a concussion."

"Why did you do it, Colin? It wasn't Shelly. He only *imagines* horrible things. It's been *you* all along!"

Colin glanced back at the crowd. I could see the embarrassment on his face. "Lindy, what are you accusing me of? You're not making sense. You've hit your head. Listen to me—"

But I was up and running now, carrying my shoes in my hands, plunging barefoot through the museum.

Did he come after me? I glanced back once but I didn't see him.

I burst out of the museum, down the steps, onto Fifth

Avenue, into the warm, fresh air and the night noise of the city, into the back of a taxi . . . and home.

"Why did it have to be Colin?" The ocean wind felt cool and soothing on my hot face. I undid my hair scrunchie and let my hair fly behind me as we walked.

"Why Colin? The only one I liked," I said, shouting over the crashing waves. "You should have seen his face. Pretending he didn't know what had happened to me. So totally innocent. But he couldn't pull it off. I could see the truth in his eyes."

Ann-Marie slid her arm around my bare shoulders and brought her face close to mine, so close I could smell the beer on her breath. "He's history," she said. "Did you call your cop friend?"

"I left a message. But I don't really have any proof, do I?"

Ann-Marie stopped walking. "Hey, I think I just saw a shooting star!"

I raised my eyes to the night sky, charcoal gray with wisps of milky clouds floating under stars, stars, stars. A silvery half-moon sat low over the ocean, lighting the waves as they crashed onto the sand.

"That's good luck, isn't it?" Ann-Marie asked, her neck still craned, eyes on the sky. "Isn't seeing a shooting star good luck?"

I sighed. "I hope so." We started walking again. "That was the *worst* party."

"Some of the guys were cute," Ann-Marie said.

"They were *kids*!" I exclaimed.

"Well . . . so?"

That evening, some guys invited us to a party a few houses down the beach. Luisa had her own plans, but Ann-Marie insisted we go, partly to take my mind off Colin and partly because she's desperate to meet new guys.

So after dinner, we trooped down the beach to the party, and at first we thought we were in the wrong house because it was all teenagers, about thirty or forty of them. The guys who invited us weren't there. In fact, we didn't see anyone over sixteen or seventeen.

Talk about a not-happening scene. Two of the guys actually asked Ann-Marie and me if we would go buy beer for them because they didn't have good fake ID's.

Not our night.

We got out of there in a hurry. Ann-Marie said we should jump in the car and go to one of the dance clubs in town. After all, we were already dressed to party. "We'll have six or seven Cosmos—my treat. Then we'll get laid, and we'll both feel better in the morning."

I laughed. "You're such an optimist."

We ended up hanging out on the beach instead. We met some guys who weren't bad. They wanted to put on wet suits and go for a night swim. But the idea made me shudder.

The waves were high that night, crashing onto shore in different directions, so we passed on the night swim. It was about ten o'clock, and we were walking back to the house to get trashed on red wine and watch some bad TV.

All the lights were on. I headed to my room.

"Maybe *The Godfather* is on," Ann-Marie called. "It's *always* on somewhere, right? I haven't seen it in at least a week."

Thinking about movies reminded me of Colin. He was so passionate about films, so entertaining and interesting. But now I even had second thoughts about that. Was his fantasy life so important to him because his real life was so screwed up?

I stepped up to the low, two-drawer dresser against the wall. I'd brought out a long, flowing cotton beach cover that would be perfect to wear now.

I slid open the top drawer. Empty.

Had I packed everything in the second drawer? I closed the drawer and tugged open the bottom drawer. Empty.

"Oh no."

My heart started to race. I suddenly felt cold all over. My clothes were gone. All of them.

"Oh no. Oh no."

Did Colin follow me out here?

"Ohmigod," I cried. "Who was here? *Who was here?*"

45

Ann-Marie came running in. "What's wrong?"

Speechless, I motioned to my empty dresser drawers. We searched the closet in my room. Then we examined the small suitcase I'd brought out with me for the weekend.

Empty. The clothes had been stolen.

Was the thief still hiding in the house?

We opened the door to Luisa's room and clicked on the light. Her clothes were tossed over the bed and strewn on the floor. Normal for Luisa. Not evidence of an intruder.

Ann-Marie crept up to her closet and slid it open. No one lurking inside.

Where was he? Waiting in the tall grasses outside my bedroom window?

"I . . . I have to get out of here," I stammered. "I can't stay in this house. Just drop me at the jitney. You and Luisa stay. I can't think straight now. I mean, I have no police protection out here. Someone was . . . in my room. Someone—"

Ann-Marie grabbed my hand. "Take a breath, Lin. You're ice cold. Let me get you some wine."

"No." I pulled away. "I have to get out of this house. I don't feel safe here."

"Come with me," Ann-Marie said. She grabbed my hand and pulled me. "Hurry."

I hesitated. "Where are we going?"

"Just follow me." She picked up a large, metal flashlight. She pulled me to the front door and then outside, and I had to run to catch up with her as she jogged toward Dune Road. Why were we going back to the beach? My head was spinning. Nothing made sense. Did she just want to get me away from the house?

She was being kind to me, I realized. She was trying to be a good friend, and I needed a friend right now.

So many weeks of fear and worry. I thought the little house on the beach was my escape. But it had all followed me out here, right to my room.

"Why did he empty my dresser drawer?" I asked, shaking my head as we jogged across the street and onto the soft, cool sand. The beach lay deserted now, except for a few fat gulls wandering in circles close to the shore, then hopping back as white foamy water lapped over the sand. "Why come all the way out here to empty my dresser drawer?"

"That's an easy one," Ann-Marie said, stopping suddenly and turning to me. "It was a warning that you weren't out of danger."

I grabbed her arm. "Please—not so close to the water."

"Sorry." She turned and we began walking across the beach, the ocean roaring to our right. She beamed the flashlight ahead of us, and we followed the darting circle of yellow light, our bare feet crunching in the cold sand.

"But who would do it? Who would follow me all the way out here?" I asked.

"I did," Ann-Marie said softly. She grabbed my wrist with her free hand. "Let's put an end to your confusion, Lindy. Let's end it once and for all. Let's take that late-night swim those guys suggested."

I stared at her, the ocean roar suddenly so loud I couldn't hear my own thoughts. "I don't understand. Ann-Marie, what are you saying?"

Her hand tightened around my wrist until it hurt, and she spun me toward the waves.

"Let go!" I screamed. "Hey—what are you *doing*? Let go!"

Her nails cut into my skin. Her grip was so tight, I couldn't free myself. She shoved me closer to the water, bumping me with her body, her eyes glowing coldly now, locked on mine, her whole face set in an angry mask.

"Did you think I didn't know about you and Lou?" she screamed, spitting the words in my face.

She gave me a hard shove toward the shore. Cold ocean water frothed over my feet, up to my ankles. My breath caught in my throat. I could feel fear taking over, paralyzing me. A tall wave crashed a few feet from me. I tried to duck away from the water, but

Ann-Marie held me in place, and the water roared over me.

"I knew everything!" she shouted. "I heard him telling you how much he loved you. How he stayed with me just to be close to you."

"But, Annie—listen—" I pleaded. "Please—"

"I *did* listen! I listened to you and Lou right outside the apartment door. I heard you both." She gave me another hard shove. I stumbled and fell, and another wave crashed over me, drenching me, soaking my hair, running down my face. I started to choke. "Annie, please—"

"Having three guys wasn't enough for you?" she cried. "You had to have my guy, too? You with your blond hair and your high cheekbones and your perfect skin. Okay, so I'm Miss Plain Jane, and you're Eye Candy. But I finally found a guy—and then you fucked me. You had to have *him,* too."

"No! That's crazy!" I screamed. "You're crazy!" I hunched my shoulders to duck under a high, cold wave. The sand swirled beneath me. Ann-Marie kept the light in my eyes.

"Yes, I was crazy!" Ann-Marie shouted, bumping me further into the water. "Crazy about Lou. But you're *stupid*. It made me laugh so hard seeing you say yes every time someone called you. It was so funny seeing you run out with these guys every night."

I gave a hard push, trying to break free, but another wave crashed over me, sending me sprawling to the sand again. Gasping for air, I struggled to my feet.

"You—" I choked out. "It was you."

She nodded, her eyes flashing in the circle of light. "You finally figured it out. See how stupid you were? Trying to blame the guys? *I* stole your underwear. *I* made the threats and pushed you into the river, and *chased* you, and *frightened* you, and—and—" She stopped for breath, her chest heaving up and down, staring at me with such hatred.

My friend Ann-Marie.

" 'Yes, yes, yes.' It was so funny to see you saying yes to them all. It was just a joke, Lindy. That's all I intended. I did it for laughs. I had so much fun seeing you in a total panic each time you had to go out with one of them. It was even worth cutting my arm. Believe me. It was such a riot. But then you had to ruin the joke, didn't you. You had to say yes to Lou, too, you slut, *you selfish slut*."

"No, you're wrong," I insisted. "Listen to me—"

But she wasn't going to listen, I knew. She was going to back me into the ocean and drown me.

"I never planned to kill you," she said. "It was just a joke. But then when I saw you and Lou snuggling together, I knew the joke had ended. That's when I decided you had to die."

"Listen to me, Annie—"

I was stalling for time. Trying to think straight, to figure out a way to save my life. But I couldn't think. Nothing made sense. I just let go—and opened my mouth in a high, shrill scream, and ran at her, my arms outstretched. Tackled her around the knees. Brought her down to the sand, wriggling and screaming.

I shoved her hard. Struggled to free my arms from around her waist.

Too slow.

I saw her hand go up. I saw the metal flashlight swing toward me.

A groan escaped my throat as the flashlight cracked the side of my head. The pain made me yelp, like an injured dog.

I couldn't see.

I couldn't get up.

I felt myself sinking, sinking into the wet sand, the water rushing over me, silent now, no sound at all, just the cold tickle of the waves as I disappeared beneath them.

46

Strong hands pulled me up. Coughing and gagging, I spit out the salty, thick water. A strand of wet weeds circled my neck. The hands untangled the weeds and pulled them off me.

Drowning, I thought . . . Can't breathe . . .

I heaved up more salty water.

Blinking, I turned to see my rescuer. Pain throbbed the side of my head. Water ran down over my eyes.

Colin?

I could make out two struggling people, wrestling on the sand. I heard their groans and angry shouts. The flashlight lay on the sand, its light pointed to the crashing waves.

Rubbing the pain at the side of my head, I climbed to my feet. I took a staggering step, then another, surprised my legs worked. I grabbed the flashlight and aimed it at the battling couple.

Colin?

No. Ohmigod. Shelly?

Shelly here on the beach?

Yes . . . Shelly. As he struggled with Ann-Marie, I could see the hospital band around his wrist.

He pulled Ann-Marie to her feet and wrapped his hands around her throat. Her mouth opened in a long horse whinny, and then she went silent. And he choked her, gleefully, triumphantly, his head tossed back as his hands worked.

"They said I can't really kill!" he shouted to me. "They said I couldn't do it for real. I could only write about it. But I can! I can!"

"Shelly, no—" I croaked, my throat raw and grainy from the salt water. "Shelly—"

He had Ann-Marie bent back over one knee, and he was strangling her, curling and uncurling his hands and then tightening them around her throat.

"Why won't the eyes pop? Why won't the eyes ever pop?"

"No!" I lurched across the sand. Grabbed his hands. Pried them off Ann-Marie's neck. And held them. Held them as she crawled away, moaning.

I gripped them tightly, the hands that had saved me. Held them between my hands. Held them so tightly I could feel Shelly's blood pulsing through his veins.

He gazed at me, calmer now, his eyes clear and bright. "Lindy, why don't the eyes pop? Why don't they pop like in my stories?"

"I'm sorry this isn't a story, Shelly," I whispered. "I'm sorry."

* * *

If this *was* a story, I guess my epilogue would take place about a month later. How did I feel? Well, *refreshed* might be a good word.

Luisa and I had a new roommate, a cousin of Luisa's from Florida who seemed nice and couldn't believe she was living in the big city. Shelly was back in Bellevue and not ready to receive visitors yet. The police were dealing with Ann-Marie, who Luisa and I guessed would soon have a Bellevue suite beside Shelly. There was even news about Dad. He was dating a woman he'd met on the Internet!

When things had settled down, Luisa and I had a few long talks about Ann-Marie. We decided her jealousy had been building up for a long time. I remembered catching her more than once gazing longingly at Ben. Did she have a crush on him? And then I remembered some problems we had at the dorm at NYU, usually after I hooked up with some new guy.

I'd always thought we were such close buddies. I guess Ann-Marie was better than I imagined at hiding her resentment.

Could I put this all behind me? Not very likely. Ann-Marie had been a part of my life for so long.

But now I walked through a crisp, sunny Monday morning in the city, a cool start to August. And yes, I felt refreshed, energized. I knew my life was starting over. I was in such a good mood, I think I was even humming to myself as I took the elevator up to the offices of FurryBear Press.

When Saralynn summoned the staff into her office, I

picked up a writing pad and my files for my book series. I had a bunch of new ideas that were certain to impress her.

Rita stopped me just outside Saralynn's office. "I'm so psyched," she whispered. "I think Saralynn is going to announce my promotion this morning."

I couldn't help myself. My mouth dropped open. I nearly gagged. "Promotion?"

"Oh. Didn't you know? Sorry." Unable to hide her grin, Rita turned and pushed open the door.

I slumped into the room filled with dread. But as it turned out, Saralynn didn't intend to talk about my series *or* Rita's promotion.

"You know that new sailboat my husband and I bought?" she said when we were all seated around the table in her office. "I'm sure you're familiar with it since it's all I've been talking about."

She gave a little laugh as if she'd just made a joke. "Well, Jake and I have decided to break it in. We're going to sail down to Tahiti and then who knows where." Her eyes were sparkling. I'd never seen Saralynn so excited.

"How long will you be gone?" Rita asked.

"Probably forever," Saralynn said, tossing back her hair. "I don't know if Jake and I will ever come back. But here's the *really* exciting news. Actually, I have good news and bad news."

She leaned forward as if to let us in on a secret. "The good news is our little company has been purchased by Random House. Isn't that exciting for FurryBear?

They paid Jake and me *so* much money to get the rights to our chubby little bear!"

"And what's the bad news?" I blurted out.

Saralynn's smile faded. "You only have till five to clean out your desks."

Actually, that was bad news and good news.

The bad news was that I'd lost my job. The good news—and it was really good—was the expression on Rita's face. She jolted in her seat as if she'd been shot in the back, uttered a soft yelp, and her face turned bright red and went through at least seventeen different expressions of horror and grief.

That cheered me up.

That evening, Colin and I were supposed to go to some Sri Lankan film he was dying to see. But I pulled him to the Dublin House, the dark, quiet bar down the block from my apartment, and I told him my news over bottles of Red Stripe. "I think that means we have to cancel our Jamaica trip," I said, holding his hands over the tabletop.

I hated to say it. We had been planning it for weeks— our first weekend away together.

Colin raised his beer. "This is as close as I'm going to come to Jamaica?"

"What can I do? I'm unemployed."

"You think you'll have trouble finding another job? With that bod?"

I pulled my hands away. "That's a totally sexist remark. I do have other qualifications."

"I know." He grinned. "But you've got it made, Lin. You're Eye Candy, remember?"

"Don't call me that!" I snapped. "I mean it." I leaned over the table and kissed him, a wet, beery kiss. "Don't ever call me that again."

"Okay. No problem. But I'm allowed to *think* it, right?"

"Don't even think—" I started. But I didn't finish because he kissed me again.